Pilgrim's Process

It was a pleasure to
meet your family!
Believe that this next
stage of life will be the
best yet!

David A. Harris, Sr.

Published by

HIS Group LLC

ISBN: 978-0-9993149-2-0
Library of Congress Control Number: 2020919777

Illustrations, cover and map by Luis Peres
www.icreateworlds.net

DEDICATION

This book is dedicated to Simone; my wife, partner, and the love of my life. So thankful we get to travel the Path of Life together.

Trail of Trials

Caverns of Zeal

The Rest of the Kingdom

Path of Life

New Country

Good Intentions

River of Life

Dove

Pit of Destruction

Thorny Thickets

Path of Life

Stealers of Seed

Familiarity Drive

City of Pleasure

Old Country

Meow

Boulevard of Broken Dreams

Lazy Lane

Path of Life

Dead End Lane

Town of Ignorance

Rocky Bottoms

Trivial Trappings

Tavern of False Fulfillment

CONTENTS

ACKNOWLEDGMENTS

A debt of gratitude is forever owed to the Ambassadors of the King that have assisted at integral parts of my journey on the Path of Life, in much the same way that the Ambassadors of the King assist Simple in this Book…

Mom and Dad, Jeff Talbert, Daryl and Margie Atwood, Gus Hunter, Robert Ewing, Joe Ewen, Jimmy Seibert, Ron Brewster, Vickie Smyer, Ruth Reese, Joe Iboji, Phil Sanderson, Ty Denning, Timothy Head, Jason Butcher, Ryan Gibson, Stewart Kelly, Robert Fuller, Cindy Jacobs, Bob Jones, Noel & Amy Tarter, Kurt and Karen Mahler, Sean and Laura Richmond, Mark and Andrea Owen, Sherri Robinson, Robert Edger, Steve Ostrom, and my good friends Aric and Juleigh Smith and Luke and Janice Whiting, just to name a few.

Special thanks to the following:

- Luis Peres for the cover art and illustrations. icreateworlds.net
- Micah Key for his assistance in proofing and editing.
- Acacia Hammond for her assistance in proofing and editing.

1

TAVERN OF FALSE FULFILLMENT

*How are they to believe in a King of whom they have
never heard? And how are they to hear without
someone sharing?*

S imple gasped in terror, jumping up from his seat
at the bar counter. Glancing around the room, he
followed the many other panicked patrons in
diving underneath the closest of the rough
wooden squared tables scattered around the room. The
whole room rattled and shook as the ground below
heaved like the earth was hiccupping from drinking its
own drought of Temporary Satisfaction. The earth
tremors only lasted about thirty seconds, but that half
minute felt like an eternity to Simple as he cowered
under the table. Tall mugs sloshed, spilling their foamy
heads as glasses skittered around the bar. Several
dropped off one by one, some crashing with the tinkle of
broken glass, while others hit the ground with loud
thumps.

Simple poked his head out like a turtle, both hands
holding tight to two of the carved legs under the wooden

table. Wasted Time, the overweight bartender, had spread eagled out over the counter, trying to save as many bottles and glasses from destruction as he could.

Who knew a man of that girth could move so quickly? Simple thought to himself. The tremors subsided just as the largest bottle on the counter fell onto the floor with a resounding thump. Wasted Time sighed with relief and wiped his cotton sleeve across his wrinkled brow and half-squinted eyes. He bent over with a thankful grunt and grabbed the blue-tinted bottle that had fallen. Its glass had been so thick it had not shattered like the others had. Wasted Time then stood back up and called out, "Looks like this one's over folks. Hop yourselves on up. Just look out for broken glass. Next drink's on the house."

Simple hesitated for a moment, making sure the tremors were over before shedding his temporary wooden shell. He finally crawled out from his hiding place and stood up. Putting both fists on his sides, he looked around wide-eyed, surveying the damage. The havoc was minimal really: a few broken bottles here and a few glasses there that had left a rainbow of darkly-colored broken glass lying on counters and floors. Mostly though, there were just spilled drinks at each customer's favorite spot.

The other bar patrons looked back and forth at each other in wide-eyed disbelief, relieved that they seemed to be fine. They nodded to Simple and raised two fingers to their foreheads in farewell as they passed Wasted Time on their way out of the bar. Wasted Time chuckled as he bid them goodbye, and said, "You all come back soon now, you hear?" as they headed home to check on the state of their affairs. They all filed out the swinging dark wood doors of the Tavern of False Fulfillment and headed down Dead End Lane to their homes in the town of Ignorance.

Simple just didn't have much to go home to, so he stayed put. A bit of light work here and there to get more money to drink and the occasional drink on credit from Wasted Time. Somehow, over time, those drinks on credit had turned into a crushing debt not likely to ever be fully paid back. This pretty much summed up Simple's existence. He knew almost everybody in the town of Ignorance and most of Wasted Time's family: Procrastination, Indecisive and a few others he'd heard stories about, such as Worries of this Life, Deceitfulness of Wealth and the mother of them all, Folly. But it was the bartender Wasted Time who did the most to keep Simple well-supplied with his favorite elixir, the draught of Temporary Satisfaction.

Wasted Time set the blue bottle down back where it went in front of the large mirror and turned back to Simple.

"Well, Simple, it looks like it's just you and me again." He smiled. "Enjoy another glass of Temporary Satisfaction. I'll put it on your tab."

Picking up a mug, he put it under the tap and filled the glass. The dark amber liquid frothed, forming a nice head. Narrowing his eyes, Wasted Time inhaled and said, "Here you go bud. Just find yourself a dry spot to sit down and don't worry about heading anywhere. If I know this town of Ignorance at all, then in no time, there will be plenty of people heading up Dead End Lane to visit us here to get their very own Temporary Satisfaction. It always happens after a shaking. Always." He chortled to himself as some private joke seemed to strike him funny.

With a nod of thanks to Wasted Time, Simple walked shakily to the back of the bar and sat at one of the only dry tables near an open window that was letting in a cool breeze. He could hear quite a cacophony of birds squawking coming from outside. "Love that beautiful music!" Wasted Time hollered from the bar. "The crows always get louder when they're about to attack. Be careful that you don't try to ever leave Ignorance, or you'll see just how bad they can be." Now that he thought about it, he couldn't remember this window ever having been open before. He looked at the ground just below the window. There was a sign that was broken into two parts now laying below the window. Ignoring Wasted Time's ramblings, he leaned down and picked up the two pieces from the ground. The smaller piece said "Lost" and the larger one said "Opportunity." Reaching out again, he hung the larger piece, which said "Opportunity" back up on the hook by the window and tossed the other piece onto the broken glass heap at one side of the room. The bartender would eventually clean it up. Then he plopped back in his seat and took a large swallow of his drink, grimacing at the taste.

Temporary Satisfaction used to be so good, Simple thought to himself. Lately, though, it had lost its luster. The froth just wasn't as cold or thick as it used to be. He had this vague remembrance of days of laughter and fun here at the Tavern of False Fulfillment, but since the time that the shakings started, nothing had seemed to be the same. Just recently, he'd had a nagging thought during one of the shakings that had turned into a bona fide craving to know what existed outside the town of Ignorance. Did people in other places experience the shakings too? His questions to other citizens of Ignorance as to what was outside the town had surprisingly resulted in outbursts of anger.

"Why would anyone care what existed outside of Ignorance?" they would say. "You're not really thinking about leaving us, are you?"

Not wanting to hurt anybody's feelings or be the cause of such animosity, Simple quelled the questions and he hadn't really pursued the topic any further.

At that moment, the dark stained wooden bar-doors swung open with a resounding crash and in came the most un-ignorant looking person, walking in the most un-ignorant kind of way.

Approaching the counter, the stranger put his booted foot on a chair rung, lowered his hood, exposing his wild, greying hair to the light and slapped his hand on the bar. Turning to Wasted Time, who was bent over again sweeping up broken glass with a wicker broom he exclaimed, "I would like a drink of Pure Delight!"

Wasted Time stood up with a succession of grunts, scowling at the stranger. "We don't serve that type of drink here sir," He said, the word "sir" as if he were tasting something nasty.

The stranger cocked an eyebrow and scratched his ear in apparent puzzlement. "Well, why not?"

"Number one, they say Pure Delight is a draught meant for the followers of our so-called 'beloved,' but nonexistent King. So it simply doesn't exist, just as the King does not exist and even if it did exist, I certainly wouldn't be serving it in my establishment. "Looking over at Simple in the back, he lowered his voice. "Plus, I hear that it actually satisfies, and I would therefore lose business, you see. Also, I hear that it's free and can't be charged for. What I do is serve just enough Temporary Satisfaction to let the patrons feel almost great, but not too good, which keeps them hungering and coming back for more. That's how I've got them trained to keep returning day after day. It's the best way to keep making money in these parts."

"Hmm, falls right in line with the typical business model for this area," The Stranger said.

He sat down on one of the stools already dried by the bartender and looked around surveying the damage in an inquisitive, perceptive sort of way, until his eyes fell on Simple. He smiled. Turning back to Wasted Time, he sketched a quick salute with two fingers to the brow, then stood up and made his way around broken glass and spills till he arrived at Simple's table. The stranger sat himself into the chair opposite Simple and flashed him a big grin, the genuine kind that goes right up and crinkles the ends of the eyes. Not knowing what to think about the stranger, Simple leaned over the table towards him and said: "Hi there, and welcome to Ignorance. My name is Simple. Who, may I ask, are you?"

The man's mouth tweaked up at both ends with an amused sort of smile.

"Well, hello, Simple," he said. "My name is Sower of Seed. My seeds are my words, and my word is my seed. As an Ambassador of the King, I've traveled here from the New Country on assignment to sow seed wherever I go. The King himself would like to invite you on a grand adventure to meet him. This mission, should you choose to accept it, is to leave Ignorance far behind and venture out onto the Path of Life. Though I must warn you, the Path of Life is fraught with troubles, trials, and adversaries of every kind. But the King has placed help of all kinds at various spots along the way to see that you make it through the Trail of Trials to successfully meet him face to face in the Caverns of Zeal."

A little cut of fear nicked Simple right at that moment in the back of his head as an invisible weight seemed to push on his chest, deep down in his heart. Sower of Seed's words frightened and excited him all at the same time. It was amazing that he had just been wondering about what lay outside of Ignorance, and here was a man claiming to be from the outside. Sweating slightly and scratching his brow, Simple said, "I'm sorry, sir, but there's no King here in Ignorance. Wasted

Time there's probably the closest thing we have to a ruler, and as I've never left this town, could you tell me more of the outside or, more specifically, who is this King?"

Sower of Seed's eyes twinkled, and his warm smile widened. "Yep, just as I thought," he said. "Simply ignorant! But that's not your fault, lad—no, not at all. Let's get you educated." His blunt words were muted by the clear affection for him that Simple could see in his face. He cleared his throat to continue:

"There has forever been one King, and there will always be one King. 'Who is the King,' you ask? Well, the King is the King. He is the King that rules the New Country as well as the Old Country. He is the King who provides Pure Satisfaction for anyone who joins him. He is even King of Ignorance, no matter what Wasted Time has brainwashed people believe. That Wasted Time is one crafty fellow and no friend to the King."

"I didn't realize all that," Simple murmured, stroking his chin thoughtfully. Running his hands through his thick hair, he considered all that he'd heard. It was finally starting to make some sense, he thought to himself, and he knew that there was something much more going on.

"As much as I would desire to go on this journey," Simple said. "Wasted Time has me in such deep debt that he would never let me leave Ignorance behind. My debt to him is so large that I could not work it off in years. He calls it my 'tab.'"

All of a sudden, Sower of Seed stood up, strode to the front of the bar, and slapped his hand down loudly for a second time. But this time, he left something behind. The bartender, who had been pretending not to listen to their conversation, jumped at the crash as something clanked loudly on the bar surface. As Wasted Time looked down, his eyes grew as big as saucers.

There was a shining golden crown sitting there. He picked it up and bit it to see if it was real; apparently, he couldn't help himself.

"That's one Royal Crown from the 'non-existent King,' and I think you'll find it more than sufficient trade to take care of Simple's debts," Sower of Seed said.

Looking Wasted Time in the eye, he pointed right at the center of his tremendous girth and said, "I declare Simple's debts to be satisfied and that he is free to be, to move, or to do whatever he chooses the rest of his life from this day forward."

Sower of Seed then turned as if he was heading for the door, but Simple spoke up:

"You look as though you're going somewhere, sir. As you've just arrived, I'd appreciate it if you would stay for awhile. You've told me of a King, and I'd like to know more."

"You will meet another Ambassador whenever you're ready," Sower of Seed said. "Just take the path that shows up and follow the signs and you just might find yourself someplace divine."

Then Sower of Seed walked right past the bartender while giving him the eye. Simple could not help but notice that Sower of Seed had neglected to give the customary two-finger salute of respect to the bartender on his way out.

"Will I see you again?" Simple yelled after him in a most un-ignorant outburst.

"Who knows what may happen on the Path of Life!" Sower of Seed shouted back over his shoulder. And just like that, Sower of Seed was out the door and gone as suddenly as he had walked in. Then, Simple heard the man's voice once more as it wafted back into the bar and growing fainter by the moment:

"Beware the birds," he called back from outside.

"Beware the Stealers of Seed."

Simple sat there for a moment—almost in shock—trying to process what had just happened. Never in all of his life had he heard of a King or of a drink called Pure Delight, and it was as though he was waking out of a deep sleep. Simple began to realize the culmination of a desire inside of him to know what life might be like outside of Ignorance, and he felt less ignorant than he had ever felt before.

A glass of Temporary Satisfaction slammed down on the wooden table in front of him. The topping of thick froth sloshed over the side as Simple was jolted from his thoughts. Simple looked up slowly and found himself looking into the threatening dark eyes of Wasted Time.

"Now, don't you worry a bit about that nonsense you just heard," Wasted Time growled. "You sit right here, have another drink and forget that guy ever came in here."

Wasted Time shuffled his bulk back across the room and behind the counter as he continued to mutter his disgust and thoughts about what the stranger had just said.

"In all my travels around the Old Country, I've never seen nor met any King. There are myths and rumors and—believe me—that's all they are. The myths say that there once was a King of all the land, but that he abandoned his post and left never to return. The rumors, propagated by un-ignorant people such as that fool say that the King is still the King and that he left only so that he could return one day and reward those who continued to follow him as King. There are other fools as well who will try to get you to leave the Old Country altogether and cross over into the New Country. They say that one day all of the Old Country will descend into darkness and be destroyed by fire and brimstone, but that somehow anyone in the New Country will be spared.

Hah! Believe me, Simple, Ignorance is bliss, and the Path of Life leads only to trouble, heartache, and pain. You've no need to discover for yourself what I know to be true. There's nothing better to do than to waste your life away right here in the good old town of Ignorance. At least you know what you can expect...more of the same!"

What? thought Simple? *New Country, Old Country, A King of all the land, Pure Delight? Why have I never heard of these before?* It was just then that Simple felt something working on his heart. Probably that seed the Sower was talking about taking root. Simple began to experience an awakening to the idea that he had to know for himself if there was something more than he had experienced so far. The sense of butterflies in his stomach rose as he realized that somewhere, out there was something called the Path of Life, and there were adventures to be had! A journey to new places, new people, and all he had to do was wait...what should he do?

Then came the horrifying realization that with Sower of Seed gone, Simple might never find the way to this Path of Life, as he was sure Wasted Time would never tell him the way. With mouth suddenly dry and palms sweaty, Simple stood up and turned towards the front door.

To Simple's surprise, Wasted Time was standing in front of the exit door. Somehow without hearing him move, the bartender had moved to block the tavern's door. And what was that click? Had Wasted Time seriously just locked the door so that Simple couldn't leave?

"I see that look in your eyes, young man" Wasted Time said. "Believe me, this is for the best. I've seen too many good young men, and women decide that there might be something better for them out there on the Path of Life, but it's not worth the hardships you'll experience. I've seen it many a time. Drink up that Temporary Satisfaction, stay here with me awhile, and Temporary Satisfaction will sure as day kill that thing in your heart that has awakened; you and I are going to continue being friends for a long time."

Looking around, Simple once again noticed the sign Opportunity by the open window. His heart leaped. Without even thinking about what he was doing, Simple sprang through the window, dropped to the ground, and took off running around the building and onto the road. There was only one way to go as the Tavern of False Fulfillment was located at the end of Dead End Lane, and so off Simple went.

**Escape from Wasted Time at the
Tavern of False Fulfillment**

2

STEALERS OF SEED

*The seeds along the path are those who have heard; then
the crows come and steal away the word from their
hearts, so that they may not believe and travel
the Path of Life.*

The hard-packed, well-travelled earth jarred
Simple's legs with each and every step as he
ran. Despite the dark clouds in the distance, a
blazing sun made his throat parched and dry
like a slightly burnt baguette pulled out of the oven. A
fear of the unknown strummed at Simple's heartstrings,
while cravings to go back to the Tavern of False
Fulfillment began.

As he dashed after Sower of Seed, Simple surveyed
his surroundings. Though he had lived in Ignorance all
of his life, it was though he was seeing the town in truth
for the first time. Receding from him at the very end of
Dead End Lane was the Tavern of False Fulfillment,
looking shabbier by the moment. The walls of that

rickety log structure cried out for a fresh painting that was long overdue, and a few shutters now hung askew from the recent shaking. How could he ever have thought it was a desirable place to spend his days?

As Simple ran, he jumped over a broken glass bottle at the entrance to a much-littered side-street, the Boulevard of Broken Dreams. This led to one of the residential neighborhoods where the inhabitants of Ignorance had chosen to dwell. The tumbledown, ramshackle and ill-cared for houses of the city were located there. Simple knew many of the dejected and lonely people who lived here. They regularly came into the Tavern of False Fulfillment for drinks of Temporary Satisfaction and for the smaller, but more potent, shots of the hard stuff—Lost Hope. Though many of the residents of Broken Dreams didn't have much money, the bartender Wasted Time seemed to thrive on extending credit and increasing their tabs. This method of increasing the financial burden of the people facilitated a cycle of dependency and reliance on the bartender and an assurance that they would never be free to leave Ignorance. Simple had been in that state himself until just a few minutes previously when Sower of Seed had opened the door to his freedom.

Dashing past the entrance to the Boulevard of Broken Dreams, Simple felt thankful that he was blessed to live in one of the nicer and better-kept neighborhoods of Ignorance. One just had to take a left on Lazy Lane, and they'd find themselves on Familiarity Drive. The residents of this neighborhood were a lot better at taking care of their homes and had regular schedules that could be depended on. The desire to go back home to what he knew on Familiarity Drive tugged at Simple's core, coaxing him to return, but a powerful new and painful yearning erupting in his heart carried him past.

The dark and ominous cloud that had previously been in the distance was now a lot nearer, and the sound of birds squawking grew louder as Simple ran. In the distance on this winding road towards the edge of town, he thought he glimpsed the wild white hair and the confident walk of Sower of Seed. He picked up his pace, anxious to catch up to Sower of Seed before this Ambassador of the King was gone forever.

As he ran down the hard beaten and dirty path, the clamor of birds swelled. The dark cloud in the distance turned, like a tornado taking shape. Simple slowed to watch in amazement at this new development happening right in front of him. Something didn't seem quite right. Butterflies in Simple's stomach fluttered until they began to feel like electricity flowing down the inside of his arms and legs. As the cloud swirled closer, Simple could see that it wasn't a cloud at all but was made up of thousands of black specks swirling closer and closer.

With each spin and twist of the cloud, the sound of birds intensified like pressure in a teapot, increasing in measure until the cacophony was an uproar of commotion. A single black-feathered fowl swooped down in front of Simple, just cresting the top of his head. At that moment, his mind then comprehended the scene in front of him as light fled, and a shadow that did nothing to cool the heat enveloped him. It was birds. Thousands of birds. Hadn't Sower of Seed said something about this flock of birds? To beware it?

A few seconds later, another fowl followed the actions of the first by skimming the top of Simple's head, claws grabbing at his hair like he was a worm that'd come out after the rain. Simple was so surprised that he slowed his running even further, his footsteps faltering to a stop as he took in the sight of the dark cloud. The black flock of ravens were now landing on the path in front and all around him. In their nearness, the uproar of the birds cawing began to take shape as each one seemed to squawk, "Seed, seed, get his seed! Seed, seed, get his seed!"

With birds on the ground ahead and behind, more and more birds entered the fray by flying around Simple in circular motions like he was the eye of the storm, the center of a tornado of movement.

As the birds drew closer, they pecked at his head, his chest, slowly driving him backwards, back the way he'd just come. The shadows around him grew thick from the flying dirt and dust that had been swept up off the hard-packed earth by the windstorm of movement of the many birds. This tempest stung Simple's eyes until he could see nothing in front of him, only a little light behind. As Simple took a step backwards, the squawking reached another decibel level. The crows that had landed on the ground began hopping excitedly, pushing Simple further and further back towards Dead End Lane, all while squawking, "Seed, seed. Get his seed!"

Simple closed his eyes against the flying storm of birds and stinging dirt and his thoughts began to grow desperate.

What if I never see the Ambassador again? Why have I never heard of the King or the fact that we're part of a bigger Kingdom? I've been told all my life Ignorance was bliss, but I've got to know what else is out there and learn more about this King.

With that last thought, Simple made up his mind to fight with a greater resolution, to push against the darkness. He hoped to glimpse some sort of gap where he could get past the birds and run down to the bend in the path after what he hoped was Sower of Seed. As he pushed forward, a renewed crush of constant attacks from the birds led instead to Simple losing his balance. As the birds swarmed him, he fell to the ground with a grunt, swinging his hands up to shield his eyes and protecting his face from the assaults of the birds.

The cloud grew darker and then even darker if that were possible. The bird's cries increased in volume, "Seed, seed, get his seed." Like black-barbed arrows, they dove and nipped at Simple's hair and clothes, overwhelming him. In a final act of desperation, Simple cried out, "Help!" Suddenly, the tenor of the crows changed from excited to angry as a ray of light broke through their gloom.

In that ray of light, a youth appeared, standing over Simple. With his left arm held aloft and guarding his head and face, he began swinging a cloak with his right arm, knocking the birds out of the way with each sweep of the cloak on his arm. Grabbing Simple by the shoulders, he hauled him to his feet, pulled his face forward till they were eye to eye, and yelled, "Follow me!"

Pulling Simple behind him, the young man swung his cloak left and right, knocking the immediate birds in front of them out of the way. Working their way forward, step by step up the path, they slowly made progress through the funneling cloud of birds. The further they went down the road, the more the funnel seemed to dissipate till it was simply a flock of birds that had lost their momentum. The cacophony of the birds changed to a lament, "Faith, Faith, No Seed, No Seed," and light began to shine as the cloud slowly lifted. The further they continued, the faster the cloud scattered until the full light of day shone down once more on these two people. The young stranger and Simple made their way down to the end of Dead End Lane, past what was left of the cloud of crows until they reached the end of the bend. There they stopped in exhaustion to take a breath. Smiling, the stranger turned to Simple and said, "You'll be safe from those birds for now."

With the fresh light that shone again, Simple was finally able to look over his rescuer. It was a mere youth that had just saved him, a skinny boy wearing dirty clothes. As the boy took his cloak off his arm and threw it over his shoulders, Simple saw that it was tattered, dirty—mostly just rags.

"Thank you so much for your help," Simple said. "You came just in the nick of time. How did you get through the flock to reach me?"

"It's great to meet you," the youth said. "My name's Faith. I'm an Ambassador of the King. I've been sent to help all who have received their seed on the good soil of their hearts, desiring to leave the town of Ignorance behind and start their journey on the Path of Life. I'm glad you lasted as long as you did! You'd be surprised at the number of people that turn back to Dead End Lane the moment they encounter the formidable flocks of Stealers of Seed. They are here to intimidate, and if they're unable to do that, then to steal the very seed that was planted in your heart before it has time to grow roots. Generally, it's those that have allowed their hearts to be hardened by anger, unforgiveness, or bitterness that lose that which has been planted and end up staying forever in Ignorance. But those who hear the word, accept it, and then by persevering retain that word, end up reaping fruit up to a hundred times what was sown in their hearts."

"It's obvious that you've met my good friend, Sower of Seed, as you can't even start this journey without having been exposed one way or another to some particularly good news! So glad that you've started the journey by taking a leap at the first Opportunity. Folks that don't move when they can often just end up with another Lost Opportunity. That first step was yours and yours alone. Despite Wasted Time's interference, you made the choice to start the journey. Now that you've started, the King will allow me to introduce myself to you. You'll find we'll not only be good friends, but our friendship is going to grow!"

"I, Faith, am the evidence of what you've been hoping for and the substance of that which you've not yet seen. Though you might not have been able to crystallize your thoughts, your heart has been longing for a righteous King, a King that will stand up on your behalf, deliver you from your crushing debt and judge righteously for you when things are not right. Wasted Time's bar tab keeping you in bondage to poverty was not right, and thanks to the generosity of the King, your debt has been paid. The attack of the crows was intended to keep you in Ignorance, but because you made the choice to take the opportunity to step out on this journey to pursue the King, I have been released to help you and can now see that you get what's needed to continue the journey."

"Your journey out onto the Path of Life is one that any must take in order to meet the King. Your plight out of the Tavern of False Fulfillment, out of the clutches of Wasted Time has brought you for the first time out of Dead End Lane and past places of Broken Dreams and Familiarity. To meet the King, you will now take the Path of Life, but you have many new adventures ahead. Rocky Bottoms, Thorny Thickets, and the City of Pleasure are just some of the places you'll pass on your journey out of the Old Country, into the New Country. In crossing the Trail of Trials and in entering the Caverns of Zeal, you will encounter your greatest tests. After you pass these final tests, you will meet the King face to face."

"Remember that while you are traveling, don't just stay on the Path of Life, but pay attention to the signs along the way and listen to the King's Messengers that you meet, and you'll learn more than you ever thought possible about the King from the most random of his messengers as they have all met the King themselves. In his own time and in this own way, the King will reveal himself to you."

"A word of advice," Faith said, "when you continue the Path of Life, you will soon encounter Rocky Bottoms, your next big test. This is a place where the enemy will exert their effort to try to stop you and there will be trouble. Just remember that the path across Rocky Bottoms is straight and narrow. Repeat after me: straight and narrow."

"Straight and narrow," Simple repeated, shifting his weight from one foot to the next.

"Remember that, straight and narrow. Stick to the middle of the road, stay straight and narrow and you'll conquer Rocky Bottoms and find yourself continuing on to the next stage of your journey!" Faith looked down the Path of Life briefly, then turned back to Simple and continued, "It was great to make your acquaintance. Although you've overcome Stealers of Seed, you're just getting started. Now I'm off, but don't worry, I plan to be back many times to grow with you on this journey, and the more we get to know each other, the better off you'll be!"

Simple and the very young and tattered Faith solemnly put two fingers to the brow and made their good-byes. It was hard for Simple to see Faith leave, as he had just been rescued from quite the ordeal. He'd gotten out of False Fulfillment, traveling past Dead End Lane and then survived the storm-like attacks of the Flock of the Stealers of Seed. Besides the burden of his mountain of debt to Wasted Time, these were the most terrifying and yet exhilarating things Simple had ever experienced before.

Yet, just like that, young Faith was gone. One moment he had been there talking, and the next, he was gone. As weird as it should have seemed to him, Simple was fine with Faith's sudden disappearance. Somehow, he had the feeling he would see Faith again very soon. He turned back to the path and walked round the bend in the road.

There, he found the beginnings of a large forest. Tall pine trees lined the path having shed their large cones, which lay everywhere. The softness of the carpet of needles was a welcome change from the hardness of the packed dirt he had just left, easing his aching feet. The aromatic scent of pine awakened Simple's senses, and he could feel that Seed in his heart reaching deeper and growing stronger with every step forward. Looking up, Simple saw that the sun was finally coming down and the large trees cast long shadows over the path. The oven-like temperatures were finally giving way to a cooler evening. Simple treaded onward on this new path, wondering about the adventures ahead when he came across a large weathered wooden sign that marked the beginning of the Path of Life. The carved and burnt words of the moss-crowned sign read:

Welcome to the Path of Life,
Pilgrim, ahead you will find strife.
Yet the next few steps is all you need
To grow in your heart that brand new Seed.

Simple placed his hand on the sign just to verify that this journey was in fact very real and not a dream sprung from his sleeping mind. He winced in pain, and his index finger came away with a small splinter, reassuring him that this was not a figment of his imagination.

It had all come together so quickly. Another shaking had occurred. He'd been wondering about life outside of Ignorance and thinking that Temporary Satisfaction didn't satisfy as much as it used to. Then in had walked

Sower of Seed. It was all too unbelievable to be a coincidence. No, Sower of Seed the Ambassador was indeed real! His debts being paid by the King was real, too! The dark storm of the Stealers of Seed attack on Simple had been very real as well—he still had the cuts and bruises to prove it. This all proved to Simple that the instructions Faith had given about staying on the Path of Life and going straight and narrow were likely real as well. Tomorrow would tell those stories; however, this day was drawing to a close and Simple was certain that he would be the better for it.

Simple smiled, took a last look at the sign that announced a whole new stage of life for him. He took a deep breath of fresh forest air and could feel stirring of life in his heart as he turned around. With once last glance back the way he came, he bid farewell to the gloomy path behind him. Then, he headed into the darkening night and onward on the Path of Life.

Attack of the Stealers of Seed

3

ROCKY BOTTOMS

*And the seeds that fell on the rock are those who,
when they hear the word, receive it with joy. But these
roots are shallow; they believe for a little while until
times get tough, then they turn back from the
Path of Life.*

The next morning, shadows grew shorter as the rising sun crested the top of the tall pines. The morning dew on the pinecones in the trees made them glitter like jewels, while the ones that littered the path gave out a satisfying crunch underfoot. The baking hot weather of the previous day had given way to cooler temperatures and crisp air under the thick shade of tall trees as the path wound ever higher and higher through increasingly rocky terrain.

What a relief to be out of Ignorance and past the flock of Stealers of Seed, Simple thought.

It was still hard to believe so much could happen in a day. All that had happened in the last day since Simple set out was more than anything he'd ever seen before in his whole life.

As he walked, Simple noticed another wooden sign, very similar to the weathered sign at the entrance to the Path of Life. This wooden sign had bits of pine needles sticking out of it where a couple of the planks were nailed together. Approaching the signpost, Simple pulled out a few of the loose needles. Leaning forward, he inspected the carved and burnt out letters, and he read aloud…

Faith reveals the road when you can't see its shape,
Stay on the path and Rocky Bottoms you'll escape.
Lift your head and hands to the sky
And you'll find help to reach the other side.

Faith did get me started the right way on the Path of Life. I wonder if the rest of this sign has to do with the straight and narrow Faith mentioned?

As the path wound around another bend, he noticed some plants in the rocky road withering as they seemed to not have roots deep enough to flourish in the rocky soil. Simple thought to himself, *Faith said straight and narrow, straight and narrow.*

Simple continued to mutter this under his breath as he walked. Along the way, he passed the entrance to another apparently seldom-traveled lane branching off to the right. Laying there on the ground at the foot of the path was a thick, shiny chain. It was still strung up on both sides of the path looped through holes in sturdy wooden posts to the right and to the left of the path, but right in the middle of the chain, a large link lay shattered. Simple frowned at it, surprised that such a well-made chain could be broken like that.

Looking into the distance and down the new pathway, Simple could see a few buildings among the among the trees. Several white tendrils of smoke curled and dissipated above chimneys as they ascended into the air. The smells of firewood and village life wafted in with the breeze. Remembering Faith's admonition to stick to the Path of Life, he turned away from the tempting sight and continued on the path he'd been told to follow. The morning's hike stretched on in relative silence until he heard the crunching of cones underfoot just ahead. A figure came into view. Simple picked up his pace, excited to talk to someone new on the Path of Life. The slender silhouette was obviously that of a girl. As he came within a stone's throw of her, the girl heard Simple and turned her head over her left shoulder to look back at him, flipping her brunette hair over one shoulder.

"Hey there!" Simple called. "What a beautiful morning to be walking the Path of Life."

The girl smiled and turned completely to face Simple. "A beautiful morning it is! I don't know if I'm a fan of all these rocks, but yes, I think it's great to be out on the Path of Life. My name is Shallow Roots. Who might you be?"

"My name is Simple," he replied. "Today is magnificent. Just yesterday, I was in Ignorance and met a man claiming to be an ambassador of the King, his name was Sower of Seed. He told me about how there's a King of all the land and how he wants to meet me. So here I am on a journey to see if it's true. Why are you on the Path of Life?"

"Well, it just so happens that I just met Sower of Seed further back on the path at a little town called Trivial Trappings," she said. "I've been there all my life, as there's a chain-gate blocking the entrance to the Path of Life. Sower of Seed came while I was outside rocking in the front yard of my house, and he told me the most amazing story about a King of all the land! It's hard to imagine that I'd lived my whole life and never heard this story. I'm so thankful that he took the time to share! My friends thought he was crazy, but I'm excited to see if it's true. I wonder if the King will give me a new outfit! I want to prove all my friends wrong, then invite them to the palace for tea. Won't they be surprised!" Shallow Roots let out a giggle and a squeal.

"The girls said I'd never make it out of Trivial Trappings because of the chained entrance, but Sower of Seed insisted we could do it and so we walked up to the metal chain gate that's about yea high." Shallow Roots put her hand down by her knee to show just about how high the gate was. "I couldn't believe it when Sower of Seed just stepped right over that chain. I mean, who'd have ever thought that you could just step over a chain blocking that path! After that, you won't believe what happened! Sower of Seed said that the chain had been put up by some guy named Wasted Time to keep people in Trivial Trappings and off the Path of Life. He also said that the King wanted everyone to have access to the Path of Life, so Sower of Seed picked up a branch and just smacked that chain. Would you believe that it just broke in two? Who'd have thought!"

"Wow!" Simple replied. "Wasted Time kept me in Ignorance through my debt to him for Temporary Satisfaction. It looks like we're both free from his traps and are headed the same way. Why don't we travel together for awhile and see what comes of this journey?"

"Sure!" Shallow Roots replied, and together they turned and continued the Path of Life, both with a little extra bounce and energy in their steps.

Simple and Shallow Roots traveled for most of the day sharing and being surprised at similar experiences they'd had growing up in Ignorance and Trivial Trappings. Towards the afternoon when shadows started getting longer, they stopped to take a short break at a creek they crossed along the way. As they drank from its numbingly cold water, Simple was refreshed and exhilarated, but Shallow Roots was upset at the mud that clung to her dress when she stood up from her drink.

After a breather, they hit the trail again to see how far they could make it before dark. The path wound ever upward, and Shallow Roots showed increasing signs of displeasure with the journey as she climbed over progressively rocky terrain. The arm of her blouse snagged a low hanging branch, and she needed both hands to lift the hem of her dress as she managed the rocks, while the fur trimming on her dress picked up cockleburs in abundance.

As the shadows continued to grow longer, they trudged onwards and upwards. Eventually, they heard people muttering and exclaiming just a short way up ahead. A few more steps took them to a peak in the path, and the trees opened up in front of them to a majestic sight. The path turned down and as far as you could see in either direction around the mountain was a sheer-faced cliff. Below it, you could hear the echoing sounds of white-water breaking over rocks far below.

At the edge of the cliff, Simple and Shallow Roots observed a crowd of people gathered looking down into the depths below. Simple and Shallow Roots traversed the short distance down the rocky path to the edge of the cliff and joined the crowd.

"What's going on?" Simple asked towards the backs of two men looking down the cliff into the chasm.

As they turned, Simple recognized the two guys standing there. They were Procrastination and Indecisive, two sons of the bartender, Wasted Time. They turned, and a mutual recognition gleamed in their eyes as they looked at Simple.

Indecisive said, "Well, well, well. Here he is now. How dare you leave Ignorance and go on the Path of Life! Have you no regard for all that our dad has done for you? He took care to make sure you had plenty of Temporary Satisfaction, even when you couldn't afford it. How ungrateful of you for not staying home instead of venturing out on this journey. Why would you even think of leaving us behind? Believe me, your trip will lead to nothing good. You definitely should have stayed at home like any good Ignorant would!"

"What are you doing here, then?" asked Simple.

Indecisive's furrowed brows clearly portrayed a look of indecision about what to say in response. Procrastination just took a step back, waiting for his older brother Indecisive to make up his mind on what to do. They looked at each other for a moment when that flicker of memory turned on like a light bulb.

Indecisive turned back to Simple, "Dad told us you would travel up the Mountain to Rocky Bottoms and for us to meet you here and to take you back home. He warned you the Path of Life was a waste of time, and so we're to bring you back home so you'll be safe. Just look here ahead at this impossible chasm, and you'll see exactly what we mean. This here is a dangerous cliff with no way across. You might as well turn back now, and let's all get on back to Ignorance."

Along with the bystanders and onlookers, everyone looked out across the gulf that separated them from the other side. They were standing at the edge of a cliff! Below roared a narrow river that flowed over and around a boulder-strewn chasm floor. However, right in the middle of the path was a narrow wooden beam that stretched from one side of the cliff to the next. Who knew how it had gotten there or when, but there it was clearly a very dangerous way across.

"Who's going to walk across that beam to make it to the other side?" Procrastination asked.

"I know I'm not. I don't think you should either," Indecisive said.

Shallow Roots and Simple looked at each other, looked at the beam, then looked down into the chasm of Rocky Bottoms below. Looking down, Simple saw that at the bottom were several unusual dark shapes.

"Do you see those bodies broken on the rocks below?" asked Shallow Roots.

Simple gasped with surprise, realizing that indeed, those shapes belonged to bodies of past pilgrims that had tried to cross.

"I didn't know the Path of Life would be so dangerous when I started this trip," Shallow Roots said. "I just thought it would be fun all the way. While I do want to meet the King to see if he'll give me a new outfit, that's not a good enough reason to take the risks of trying to cross that beam across the chasm. I'm going to head back to Trivial Trappings if Procrastination and Indecisive here will take me on their way back to Ignorance. I think you should go with us."

Simple noticed some dry, dying plants in the shallow rocks on the side of the ravine and heard the distant caws of crows while he considered his predicament. He reflected on his previous conversation with Faith.

Faith did tell me I'd be tested with trouble at Rocky Bottoms, and he told me to stay straight and narrow, and to pay attention to the signs along the way. The sign said, 'Faith reveals the road when you can't see its shape. Stay on the path and Rocky Bottoms you'll escape. Lift your head and hands to the sky and you'll find help to reach the other side.'

Simple began thinking to himself furiously, *If I'm to conquer Rocky Bottoms and get on with my journey to meet the King, I'm going to have to take a step of faith, stay straight and narrow, rely on faith and trust that somehow, I'll make it across. What's the alternative? If I stop now instead of moving forward, I don't have any choice but to go back with Procrastination and*

Indecisive all the way back down the path to Dead End Lane. Getting away from Wasted Time again will be impossible now that he knows my desire to leave Ignorance behind. I barely even made it past those Stealers of Seed. I don't think I can go through all that again.

While everyone else peered down over the edge of the cliff and speculated about those that had fallen before, the sound of the crow's screeching increased. As a counterpoint to their cacophony, Shallow Roots again made it clear that she had no interest in trying to cross Rocky Bottoms.

"I'd rather be Trapped in Triviality forever and be an Ignorant Ignoramus rather than attempt to cross over Rocky Bottoms to continue the Path of Life," she kept saying.

Simple could feel the seed that had been planted inside his heart pushing past some harder, deeper places in his soul. The result was a boldness and confidence he had not experienced before. Though he was afraid, the terror that he'd previously had was draining away. To everyone's surprise and astonishment, Simple pushed past Procrastination and Indecisive and stepped up to the edge of the cliff facing the wooden beam.

"If there really is a King and he's good, then it's worth it to face this danger to pursue the truth," said Simple as he took his first step out onto the beam. He froze only for a second, then took his second step, and then his third. Against his better judgement, Simple looked down at the dark bodies broken on the rocks below. He wondered what the story was of these pilgrims who had gone this way before and fallen. Lifting his head back up, he caught sight of the flocks of Stealers of Seed in the distance. Much to his despair, they were circling towards him. Fear crept up again. From behind him, he heard Indecisive's condescending voice calling out: "You can still come back; it's not too late. I'm sure our dad will forgive you for wasting all of our time on this foolish journey of yours."

Indecisive's whining voice came across as so condescending to Simple that it had the opposite of its intended effect. Instead of causing him to drawback, it served to motivate him forward. With a heat of anger, he took two more steps just out of spite. Suddenly, an unexpected breath of wind caused Simple almost to lose his balance. He waved his arms in circular motions trying to regain his stability.

My King, what have I gotten myself into? thought Simple in a terrified internal whisper.

"My King, help!" escaped his lips.

He began tilting in the direction the wind was blowing, the same direction the crows were flying towards him from, and now he could hear the loud, intimidating caws even louder.

In that moment, Simple remembered the words of the sign once again: "Lift your head and hands to the sky, and you'll find help to reach the other side."

In desperation, Simple lifted his chin to the sky, and with incredulity, saw something he hadn't noticed before.

Everyone had been so intent on the broken bodies at the bottom of the ravine that they didn't notice the two ropes hanging to the right and left of the beam. The ropes, tethered at both ends to treetops, were camouflaged from the onlooker's view. Simple reached up and grabbed first the rope on the right, regaining his balance, then the rope on his left. In an instant, he felt so much better.

He continued his trip over the beam, crossing Rocky Bottoms with his hands up in the sky, grasping the ropes the whole way. The black multitude of crows seemed to have just disappeared into thin air. As Simple progressed, he was relieved to see that the beam in fact became wider and wider as he went across, a feature of this bridge which also couldn't be seen from the other side. At the end of the beam, Simple hopped up onto the dirt path, safe once again, elated that he'd overcome his fear concerning falling into the chasm at Rocky Bottoms.

Without warning, Faith stood before him again. "Way to go, Simple!" Faith said.

Shaking his head with a mixture of relief and surprise, Simple asked, "Where did you come from?"

Faith replied, "I'll always be around every time you decide to move forward on the Path of Life. You might not always see me, but as long as you're moving forward, I'm always here and helping behind the scenes! You did well to look up like the sign said. Some pilgrims get past Procrastination and Indecisive just to spend their time looking down at the danger. Even though they take a few steps forward, they ultimately lose their balance, fall off the path and are bashed to pieces on Rocky Bottoms."

While Faith was talking, Simple looked at him more closely. Something seemed different about his friend. Though he was still skinny, his face seemed to have a fuller, ruddier complexion than he had the first time Simple had seen him. The tattered and rugged cloak had also been replaced with a new, stronger material.

"Now your next trial will be just ahead," Faith continued. "Remember, no matter what anyone says, just stay on the Path of Life and keep moving forward!"

Faith put two fingers to his brow in salute, and just as quickly as he had appeared, he was gone.

Looking back across the chasm at Rocky Bottoms, Simple felt both sadness as he saw Shallow Roots turn her back and head back the way she had come as well as relief as Procrastination and Indecisive turned back as well.

Though they weren't looking at him to notice, Simple sketched a quick farewell salute to them, then turned and continued on the Path of life.

Simple Crosses Rocky Bottoms

4

THORNY THICKETS

And as for seed that falls among the thorns, they are those who hear, but as they go on their way they are choked by the Worries of Life and Deceitfulness of Wealth, and their fruit does not mature.

The next morning, before the sun crested the treetops, Simple got up and dusted his pants off. Grateful for another day on the Path of Life, he continued his walking journey, breathing in the brisk morning air as the path wound down from the heights of the mountains. The trees changed from needle pines to the leafier oaks with their pock-marked grey trunks. At this elevation, the forest was also more open and airy, alternating with heavy and thick sections, and in some places, large vines crisscrossed the path. As Simple walked, he noticed a particular vine that was thick with wicked-looking thorns.

I'd hate to accidentally walk into one of those, Simple thought.

He noticed an object on the side of the trail just up ahead. As he came closer, he saw that here was another weathered sign. Like the others, the oak wood had carved out and burnt words:

Worries of Life and Deceitfulness of Wealth
Seek to choke you with their stealth.
Go on instead, save your breath
Or you'll find yourself in the Pits of Death.

After reading the sign, Simple scratched his head and thought to himself: *Interesting. I wonder what adventures this will bring*? Whatever it is, I bet the King's provided a way through just like he has before."

He turned and continued on down the road. It was a rather pleasant walk for most of the morning until the sun was directly overhead. It was then that Simple ran into an anxious-looking man with worry wrinkles across his forehead and crows' feet around his eyes.

Simple heard a crow caw in the distance as the man began talking with an air of desperation.

"Oh my boy. Don't continue on this path!" the man said, his eyes wide in fear. "My name's Worries of this Life, and I'm worried for your safety! There's a lion in the road up ahead. If you keep going, you're sure to be eaten and torn apart into a million pieces!"

"A lion in the road? Oh no! What do I do?" Simple asked, his own concern furrowing his brows.

"You don't have any choice but to go all the way back to Ignorance. Anything else would be foolish!"

Simple stood there for a minute and considered the ramifications of going back to Ignorance. With a flash of insight, Simple asked, "If we wait just a bit, won't the lion move on and we'll go on down the path?"

"Why risk the chance?" Worries of Life said. "I've been here for months warning people about the lion, and everyone else has been smart and turned back. Why don't you be smart like them and turn back to Ignorance?"

Again, Simple pondered Worries of Life's words. "Wait a minute here," he said. "You said, 'months.' You've been here for months telling people to turn back?"

"Yes, that's right, and you'd be smart to heed my words. There's a nasty end waiting to any who continue on this path!"

"When was the last time you saw this lion?" Simple asked.

"What does that have to with anything? I've never seen a lion in my life, and for that matter, I hope I never will! My uncle told me to tell everyone that there was a lion on the Path of Life up ahead and you know if you think about it, there's got to be a lion somewhere, why not up there? So, you might as well go ahead and turn around and save yourself some wasted time while you still can."

Simple pondered the words to himself. A picture in his mind was beginning to emerge. "You've never seen a lion...your uncle told you...wasted time? Wait a minute, who's your uncle? It wouldn't by any chance be Wasted Time from the town of Ignorance would it?"

"Well, of course, it is though I do say I've no idea how you knew it was him."

"Well, doesn't that just make a lot more sense! I thought I was done with him, but here he is still trying to get me back to Ignorance. Thank you, but no thank you. I'm just going to go ahead and continue on my trip down the Path of Life, thank you very much."

Simple pushed past Worries of Life and continued on his merry way. He traveled a few more quiet and pleasant hours. The only thing he saw that even somewhat resembled a lion was a ginger tomcat with a particularly fuzzy neck. The cat skittered away when he saw Simple coming.

As he continued down the path, Simple came to an unusual-looking man who flashed him a big pearly white smile. The man's bright green jacket sparkled in the sunlight and covered an equally loud red shirt. The man's yellow bow tie clashed with the whole outfit in a way that said the wearer was large and in charge.

"Well, hello there," the man said. "My name is Deceitfulness of Wealth. I already know that you and I are going to be great friends! Where are you headed this beautiful afternoon?"

"I'm traveling the Path of Life," Simple replied. "I come from Ignorance, where I met Sower of Seed, one of the King's Ambassadors. He told me a story I'd never heard about a King of all the land. I'm now traveling the Path of Life to meet him. Do you know the King?

Deceitfulness of Wealth's nose wrinkled in a funny sort of way, and he responded, "Do I know the King? I know everybody! The King hasn't been around here in quite some time though—" then muttered under his breath, "—thankfully." He continued on, "I see that you're a traveler, and it's a good thing for you that I'm here because I'm going to help you on your journey. You see, I once was a traveler just like you, and that was when I discovered the City of Pleasure just up ahead. Little did I know it at the time, but the City of Pleasure can be a lot of fun. Of course, that only happens if you have money. You'll need money for food, money for a place to stay—everything there happens with money."

"Now, first, I tried to get money the difficult way by working hard, but that's so strenuous, tiring, and wearying, and then you have to save your money and ration it over time—who wants to wait that long to live the good life? My dear old uncle used to tell me, 'Don't waste your time working hard to earn money. If you want money, find a river where the money's flowing, go out and stand in the middle of that river, and take it!' Well, this here path is my river and there are loads of travelers, who unlike yourself, actually travel with plenty of money. All we have to do is waylay one of those hapless souls, and take what they have, then we're living the good life!"

Deceitfulness of Wealth then turned and pointed to a fork in the road up ahead.

"Just follow me this way—and trust me, it's fun. When we're done you'll have plenty of money for all that you need and more!" The Path of Life led obviously to the left, but the way Deceitfulness of Wealth was pointing looked to be in the same general direction.

Wow, thought Simple. Deceitfulness of Wealth is so intriguing and so charming! It was hard not to be swayed by such a confident fellow.

Simple began thinking to himself: *You know, I've not seen Faith since Rocky Bottoms and it would be so nice to have somebody to walk with for awhile. If I go with Deceitfulness of Wealth I'll not only have someone to talk to, but maybe I can make enough money to stay someplace nice at the upcoming City of Pleasure he just told me about.*

So, off Simple went with Deceitfulness of Wealth to the fork in the road. Simple noticed that the fork was very dark with large trees and low hanging branches right over the intersection of the two paths.

"OK, Simple, this is how we do it," Deceitfulness of Wealth said. "Notice the newer path and how dark it is? We put this path here as a decoy for the real Path of Life. Because the fork in the road here is new and unexpected, everyone always stops and looks at the new path to get their bearings and make sure they're going the right way."

Deceitfulness of Wealth walked over to the large tree and pulled out a bundle that was hidden underneath branches and leaves.

"We're going to spread those nets out here all over the path. As it's getting dark, travelers won't even see them. We're going to climb up into that tree with the low hanging branches. Up there, there the vines will be connected to the nets here on the ground. Whenever travelers stop to look where they're going, we're going to jump down, pulling the vines and the nets will come up entangling the traveler, and we'll waylay that unlucky one and take everything they have. Then, we'll disappear into the forest down the dark path to divide up and split the loot."

Simple knew immediately in his heart that this plan was wrong, but if he didn't participate, what was he going to do about money in the City of Pleasure? He had nothing for food or shelter, and his sandals were sure getting worn. We probably won't actually hurt anyone, he rationalized, so he decided to go along with it and see how it went.

The sun was on its downward slope, so they spread out the net all over the ground beneath the large branches. They connected vines from the tree to each end of the net just as Deceitfulness of Wealth had planned. It seemed very much likely that when a traveler stepped onto the net that they would be able to catch him unaware by pulling on the vines. Both Simple and Deceitfulness of Wealth ascended the tree, climbing up to just the right spot out on the wide branches. After adjusting several times to get comfortable and situated before the shadows grew too long, they settled down to wait. As he was climbing up, Simple painfully pierced his hand on a thorn. As he looked around, he noticed that there were quite a few vines covered in thorns wrapped around the tree. If it weren't for the thicker clothes he was wearing, Simple was sure he would be in much worse shape.

Simple and Deceitfulness of Wealth were perched next to each other on one of the more particularly leafy lower hanging branches. From this vantage point, they could not be seen. Each of them held one of the two vines at the ready in their hands. It was then that Simple realized the vines holding the net were the same type of vines wrapping the tree and covered in thorns. Simple leaned over to point this out to his companion, but was silenced by a quick finger to the lips and then a point down the road.

Simple heard the traveler before he saw him. It was a middle-aged man. Just as Deceitfulness of Wealth had said, the traveler came to the fork in the road and stopped directly on top of the open net. He peered down the new lane, then shrugged as he turned to continue on the Path of Life.

"Now!" yelled Deceitfulness of Wealth. He began pulling the vine as hard as he could. At that exact moment, as the tension on the vine grew tight, Deceitfulness of Wealth discovered the thorns on the vine. He screamed in pain as the many thorns pierced both of his hands. Deceitfulness of Wealth was so surprised at the pain that he lost his balance and fell headlong to the ground. The crunching impact of Deceitfulness of Wealth hitting the ground head first sent shivers up Simple's spine. The middle-aged traveler looked at Deceitfulness of Wealth's crumpled body wonderingly, then shading his eyes, gazed up into the tree trying to make sense of what had just happened. Simple, horrified at the thought of what might happen if he were caught, held his breath, and prayed that he would not be seen.

44

The traveler looked up right at Simple and said, "Not much point in spreading a net in full view, where even all the birds can see. Come on down here, young man, and let's get a look at you!"

Climbing down the thorn-ridden tree was much harder than going up. It was as if all the thorns had been quite happy to see him ascend the tree, and now that they had Simple in their grasp, they were attacking him with a vengeance all the way down. Though scratched and bleeding on his hands, arms and legs, Simple eventually made it to the bottom.

"Well, young man, my name's Good Samaritan," the traveler said. "It's a good thing for you that I happen to have a habit of caring a lot about people like you who fall into trouble, but don't even know they're in it. Unfortunately for Deceitfulness of Wealth here, it's a little too late. Let me help teach you a lesson you will hopefully never forget. Follow me."

Good Samaritan bent and checked on Deceitfulness of Wealth's body. Just as Simple expected, he pronounced him definitely dead. Good Samaritan picked up the deceased body and slinging it over his shoulder, he took Simple up the new path. The path grew darker the further in they went, a gloom which seemed to be a combination of the lateness in the day as well as the thickness of the foliage overhead.

"Deceitfulness of Wealth thought that he built this path, but the truth is it has been here for many generations," Good Samaritan said. "Many in his line have used this as a place of ambush for unwary pilgrims on the Path of Life. All in his family are deceivers, thieves, and robbers who care only about themselves and getting rich quick at other's expense. You likely met one of Deceitfulness of Wealth's brothers Worries of Life on your way up here. Worries of Life and Deceitfulness of

Wealth often work hand in hand to bring down anyone they can."

At this point, they reached an enormous dark pit in the road.

"This path is called the Path of the Dead, and this is the Pit of Destruction," Good Samaritan said. "There are several paths to this pit coming from various directions. One of the biggest ones comes out of the City of Pleasure."

Simple looked over the edge of the pit into the darkness, but could not see the bottom. Wrinkling his nose at the sickly smell in the air, he asked, "What is that smell?"

"That's the 'wonderful' fragrance of death and destruction," Good Samaritan said. "This pit is the end to all who go after ill-gotten gains."

As his eyes adjusted to the gloom, Simple began to see protrusions in the darkness of the pit, with bleached white objects at the top. Is that a skull? Simple thought to himself. Then it became apparent that some of the protrusions were skeletal remains of legs or arms, poking out of the gloom below.

Standing there at the edge of the pit, Good Samaritan shifted and slid the body of Deceitfulness of Wealth from his shoulder to the crook in his arms. Then, carefully, with a sigh of regret, allowed the body of Deceitfulness of Wealth to slide into the Pit of Destruction.

"It's a shame that it has come to this, but such IS the end of all who go after ill-gotten gain, "he repeated. "If you had been successful in ambushing me or another pilgrim on their journey, then Deceitfulness of Wealth would have brought you back here, thrown you into the pit, and kept all of the loot for himself. Plans to work with him never turn out the way you expect. Now let's get out of here before it gets completely dark."

Turning back, Good Samaritan headed up the path, back the way they'd come. With one last look and a cold shiver that went down Simple's spine, he turned back and followed Good Samaritan until they reached the fork in the path Deceitfulness of Wealth had led him to.

"If you'll continue on this path, you will come to the City of Pleasure just up ahead before it gets dark," Good Samaritan said.

"Would you mind walking with me there? "Simple asked. "I'm concerned as to what I'll do once I get there. I don't have any money, so I don't know what I'll eat or where I'll stay once I'm there. That's the reason why I was working with Deceitfulness of Wealth down the Path that led to the pit."

"Unfortunately, I can't go there right now," Good Samaritan said. "The King has assigned me a task, and it's my pleasure to obey. For a season of time, I'm monitoring the path between Rocky Bottoms and the City of Pleasure. Sower of Seed has been particularly effective, so we're in a season of more pilgrims walking the Path of Life. There are many enemies of the King whose only goal is to waylay poor souls and see them fail on their journeys. Wasted Time's gotten many of his relatives out in force to stop any and all they can from completing their journey. Just head on towards the city. Don't forget that the King is a good King, and it's his pleasure to take care of his subjects. You might just find yourself in a better position that you expected."

Giving Simple a firm handshake, Good Samaritan turned and headed back up the path. Simple stood there thinking about what had happened and what Good Samaritan had said.

The King takes good care of his subjects. Am I one of his subjects, or is there something I have to do to become one of his subjects? Simple wondered. I'm sure one day soon I'll figure it out. I hope the King is not mad at me for what I just tried to pull with Deceitfulness of Wealth.

Simple turned and continued on his Journey down the Path of Life.

A Thorny Trap is Laid

5

CITY OF PLEASURE

*Does not Wisdom call out? Does not Understanding
raise her voice?
On the heights beside the way, at the crossroads she
takes her stand;
beside the gates in front of the town...she cries aloud...*

*"Whoever is simple, let him turn in here!" To him who
lacks sense she says, "Come, eat of my bread and drink
the wine of Pure Delight. Leave your simple ways, and
live, and walk in the way of Insight."*

The sun rose higher and higher as Simple walked along the hard-packed dirt of the Path of Life, thinking about the journey thus far.

I can't believe I almost ended up in the Pit of Destruction, Simple thought to himself. *I'm so glad Good Samaritan was assigned to help travelers journeying the Path of Life.*

It was then that Simple came across another sign, and he stopped to read.

Two voices in the city that you'll hear
Wisdom's and Folly's, both loud and clear
Life or death, they will contend,
Which one you follow determines your end.

Life or death, wow, that's big! Simple thought. *Just nearly ended up in the Pit of Destruction, so I for sure want the wisdom to find life on this journey. I hope I find it quickly in the city.*

Simple continued on the Path of Life, thinking about his journey, both what he'd already seen and what might lie ahead. It was not much time at all until his path took him out of the forest and through a broad pasture. He looked up, and there before him was the City of Pleasure. The city did not have any walls per se, but large buildings bordered it with many paths in and out. The Path of Life did not branch out to those openings, but instead wrapped around until it came to a large gate at the front.

It was there, at the front of the city's gates, where Simple thought he heard someone call his name.

"Simple! Hey Simple, over here!"

Simple turned in the direction of the voice, and there before him was a short, heavier-set lady with hair the dirty white and grey color of a sheep.

Pointing at his own chest, Simple asked, "Are you talking to me?"

The lady wagged her finger at him. "Well, who else would I be talking to? Your name is Simple, isn't it?" She said the last part as a statement rather than a question. "Come on over here and let me have a look at you." Without thinking, Simple found himself obeying her summons, presenting himself for her inspection.

"You are the spot-on description that Sower of Seed described to me," she said. "You've got a little way to go before you lose that look of Ignorance, but at least you're on your way…better late than never, right?" she stated with a smile. "Sower of Seed is a good friend of mine, and we always visit when he's passing through. He just crossed the border over to the New Country earlier this morning. There is need of seed sowing even there. Well, come on and let's go."

And off the lady started walking through the gate and into the city.

"Wait!" Simple cried out, but when it was obvious that this older lady was not stopping and that she would leave him behind if he didn't catch up, Simple went ahead and followed behind like a puppy following his master.

"Come on to my house, and I'll put you up while you're here in the City of Pleasure to help keep you out of trouble. I've got a table laid out and a special bottle of Pure Delight ready for you. I'll introduce to you to Prudence, who lives with me. She is really great to keep around. She stays right on top of things. Knowledge and Discretion were over at the house when I left it earlier, but I think they're pretty busy for the next few days thanks to Mr. Intellectual. You've got to know them if you're going to spend any time in the City of Pleasure so as not to get wrapped up with the likes of that floozy Adulteress and others. You'll definitely meet Understanding, and if you're lucky, you might just meet his twin Insight. You never know with that girl, Insight. She has a way of popping up at the most bizarre and unexpected of places, though it's always great when she does. Oh yes, by the way, my name is Wisdom, and I'm pleased to make your acquaintance," she said with a nod to Simple. "We need to get home as it's almost twilight," she added as Simple shuffled behind her.

Simple followed this woman down the broad dirt roads, allowing her words to wash over him. He figured that if she were friends with Sower of Seed, then she was probably all right. Besides, his stomach was growling, and he couldn't remember the last time he'd had a decent meal. Not only that, but Simple was simply antsy with anticipation of a glass of Pure Delight. Ever Since Sower of Seed had planted that seed in him back at the Tavern of False fulfillment on Dead End Lane, he'd not forgotten about it and was bubbling with anticipation. So, for now, Simple dutifully followed.

"Now we're passing one of the highest points in the city," Wisdom said as they turned a corner. Sitting in a dirty, rickety wooden chair outside a ramshackle of a house that was in need of repair was another older lady with unruly black hair and disheveled clothes. As they walked past, she looked Simple up and down, sending shivers down his spine. He wrinkled his nose at the stale scent of death in the air.

"Hey there! Simple, you come here."

Startled, Simple stopped and looked at the woman sitting there, knowing for sure he did not know who she was, though there was a familiar air about her.

"Pay Folly no mind, she'll waste your time any chance she gets,' Wisdom said, turning her head back to Simple. It was then that Simple knew who the woman sitting outside that house was.

In a loud cackling, boisterous voice, the black-haired lady said: "That's right. I know exactly who you are. You left my son Wasted Time behind, and he's wasted a lot of time on you making sure you had a good time in Ignorance. Too bad you up and left him the first time you got a teensy, weensy little seed. Wasted Time's stopped many a person from receiving their seed. And the ones that do get out of False Fulfillment, don't usually make it to the end of Dead End Lane by the time that flock of crows, Stealers of Seed get done. He'll never forgive you for leaving Ignorance behind. And my grandsons Procrastination and Indecisive—how rude of you to barely even stop and talk to them! Anyone who takes the time to get to know them will turn right on back to where they came from, just like that good little girl Shallow Roots. She'll never leave Trivial Trappings behind. I'd best my last drink on it. That seed of faith must have really started growing in your heart for you to cross Rocky Bottoms." Putting her head down, she muttered to herself, "I never figured how anyone could get over that chasm."

Raising her head back up again, she said, "Well, I've got my eye on you. Hey, you don't have any of that Temporary Satisfaction, do you?"

Simple shook his head slowly from side to side.

"No? What about some food?"

Again, Simple shook his head.

"No! It doesn't look like you have much of anything do you? Well, if you happen to find any food or drink, help an old lady out and bring it back here and we'll go inside and reminisce about what you've left behind. I usually expect Deceitfulness of Wealth to show up by now and share his plunder with me, but for some reason he hasn't shown up this evening. I wonder where he's off to."

Leaning in, Wisdom grabbed Simple by the cuff and said, "Pay Folly no mind."

"You mind your own business, Wisdom," Folly interrupted. "Just because you have Prudence taking care of your place, don't you go get all high and mighty on me."

"You know where I live, Folly. Anytime you want a drink of Pure Delight, you come on down, and we'll get you fixed up."

"Blah blah blah, Pure Delight my foot. That nasty concoction is for King followers, of which I'm not. Besides, I heard there's a lion in the streets. I'm gonna stay right here where it's safe."

Looking up and glaring at the both of them Folly yelled at Simple, "Come into my house or move along!"

Simple and Wisdom looked at each other and continued walking down the road. Suddenly, Simple coughed and began rubbing his nose.

"What was that smell?" he asked Wisdom.

"The dead are there with Folly. She's built her house right on the edge of the Path of the Dead and not too far from the Pit of Destruction, just like that floozy Adulteress—well, speak of the devil, there she is now. "

The darkness was just reaching twilight. There, near the corner of the street was a woman with her face painted white, darkened eyes, and extended eyelashes. She was walking slowly in a very deliberate swaying motion, intentionally getting nowhere fast. Wisdom quickly crossed over to the other side of the road, and Simple followed her. Even with a street in between them and Adulteress, the thick scent of myrrh, aloe, and cinnamon wafted over to them. The odor seemed like someone was trying to drown out the smell of death, though not very successfully. The thickness of it overwhelmed Simple's senses, making him almost dizzy.

At that moment, a young man was passing by. Adulteress grabbed him by the front of his shirt, brazenly pulling him towards her. Even with the background sound of the cackle of crows increasing, Simple could still hear her words as she said to him, "Today, I've been a good girl and have fulfilled all of my vows. My husband's just left and has taken a full month's worth of traveling supplies with him. Now, I have all of this food at home and no one to share it with. I'm so lonely and just can't bear to be alone. Come, keep me company tonight!"

The young man initially resisted her advances with various weak excuses, intending to continue on the way he was going, but she just wouldn't let him go. Finally, he just gave up, turned, and followed her past the burning brazier and up a flight of stairs like a cow going to be slaughtered. When Adulteress opened the door to her wooden house and led the young man in, Simple began wheezing and sneezing at the overpowering stench of death mixed with spices.

Moving on, Wisdom and Simple walked till they came to a new district in the city where the houses were much more well kept and made of granite and stone. They approached a large structure where Simple counted seven large gleaming white pillars out front. Entering the door of that large house, they were met by a servant boy holding a silver tray with a fluted flask and cups. Wisdom picked up the silver flask engraved with interweaving patterns and poured a steaming red drink into two of the small cups. Handing one of the glasses to Simple and taking one for herself, she said, "Cheers!" She then threw back the drink in a single gulp and returned her cup to the tray.

"Thank you, darling," she exclaimed, smiling broadly, to which the servant boy bowed his head.

Simple sipped the heated spiced wine, and a strong warmth filled his body, starting with a tingling sensation in his mouth that went down into his stomach and radiated outwards till his skin was flushed, as if he'd been sitting by a large fire. A previously unrecognized tension of the journey thus far began easing away as Simple became aware of the simple significance of the present moment. It was as though he'd always been living for the next moment or for a day that might come in the future, but right now, he just wanted to sit and bask in the richness of the moment.

"Wow, what a drink!" he found himself saying aloud with a gasp of joy.

"That, young man," said Wisdom, "is Pure Delight. It's good both warm or cold, in good company or alone. This is a special draught that's given to us by the King. It helps brings you into the reality that right here, right now, everything is going to be all right! Just one of many gifts the King loves to give his subjects. Amazing, isn't it, how this delight that is the richest of fare can be purchased without money and without cost! All that's needed is the simplicity of slowing down enough to enjoy it! Go on in through that door into the sitting room up ahead and sit down in front of the fireplace, and I'll go round everyone up so that you can meet the family."

Passing through the open wooden door into the main sitting room, Simple found several cushioned sitting chairs spread out in a half-moon around the hearth. Just to the right was a bookshelf displaying book bindings of every color. A tapestry of complex designs and many hues lined the other walls, speaking of an appreciation for the intricacies of art and beauty.

Simple made himself comfortable in a red-cushioned chair and reveled in his continued experience of Pure Delight. In a short while, Wisdom entered the room with four people in tow: three girls and a servant boy. The first girl who stepped up had long, brown hair tied back in a ponytail. With a sharp look in her eyes, she looked to be a strong person that would be able to get things done.

"Let me introduce you to my younger sister, Prudence, the caretaker of this establishment," Wisdom said.

"Pleased to meet you," said Prudence. Her forehead was slightly wrinkled with experience, and the corners of her mouth upturned in a knowing, congenial sort of way as if she already knew all about Simple and was happy and amused with what she knew.

"This is my daughter, Discernment," Wisdom said, gesturing to the next woman in line. Discernment nodded at him, and Simple saw that although she was quite a plain and ordinary sort of woman, the keen look of her eyes seemed to be putting him on a balance and weighing him.

"Last but not least, these are the twins, my nephew, the very reliable Understanding and my niece, the unpredictable, but very enjoyable, Insight."

Up stepped the servant boy and a girl, who were both about a head shorter than Simple. Both had bleached blond hair and bright blue eyes. It was obvious that they both were likely quiet types, but when listened to could explode and overwhelm you with whatever was near and dear to their hearts. Insight giggled quietly and Understanding smiled broadly and their gleaming eyes were filled with energy as they both greeted Simple.

After meeting Wisdom's family and friends, Understanding led Simple through the house to go to his room. On the way to his room, they passed through a doorway into which a large tree was growing up from the floor. It was so large it reached up through a space in the roof. Simple tried to keep his mouth shut, but failed as he gasped at the size of the tree. The stairs circled the room where the tree was located and up those those stairs they went around the tree till they reached the upper landing and headed to one of several doors.

Understanding opened the door and Simple entered to find that a colorful room had been prepared for him, complete with a very soft-looking bed, an armoire, a cushioned wooden chair and a stand next to the bed. On that stand was a large platter of food that had been laid out, as well as a golden bell. Without warning, Simple's stomach growled loudly and embarrassingly as his body reminded him of his hunger.

"Make yourself comfortable and just ring the bell if you need anything at all," Understanding said.

"I'll probably just eat and take a nap." Simple replied.

"Sweet dreams!" a young quiet female voice behind him chirped. Startled, Simple jumped. Turning quickly, he saw that Insight had somehow entered the room with Understanding. A mischievous smile glowed on her face. Both Understanding and Insight put two fingers to the brow and then left, shutting the door behind them.

Turning back to the platter, Simple began devouring the food and drank the glass of wine that had been set out for him. He walked to the window and looked out onto the City of Pleasure. People walked up and down the dusty road headed about their lives. Simple wondered about how both Folly and Wisdom lived here in this place as they seemed such opposites. Wasted Time's family sure seemed to be everywhere, but for that matter, so did servants of the King. Interesting how all that worked.

Simple kicked off his shoes and sat on the back of the bed to think. It was hard to believe that just the day before he had been so worried about finding a place to sleep and food to eat that he had taken up with Deceitfulness of Wealth. He'd been willing to steal and entrap someone else just to take care of himself. If he'd been successful, he would have found himself in the Pit of Destruction; he was sure of it. Thankfully the King's ambassador, Good Samaritan had come along and not someone else who could have done who knows what to him.

The King must be really good to have these types of ambassadors and then allow him to move on down the path so quickly from so great a mistake. Simple looked down at the scratches on his hands from climbing down the tree with thorns and saw that they were healing nicely.

Then he looked over at the tray of food, and was momentarily surprised to find it empty, except for a few crumbs. His eyes began to droop, so he pulled down the coverlet, and then lay down on the large comfy bed with his head on the thick pillow. He wondered how long he would be here in the City of Pleasure before returning to the Path of Life, but before he could finish that train of thought, quickly fell asleep as the afterglow of Pure Delight still permeated his senses.

Wisdom's House

6

RUMOURS OF DESTRUCTION

They know neither the day, nor the hour.

Some time later in the night, Simple woke up with a start and sat up, rubbing his eyes. Through the darkness in the room, he knew it was still nighttime. Yet he was restless and unable to go back to sleep. He got up, walked across the floor to the window, and looked past the curtains. Gazing out at the cobblestoned streets, he saw by the many torches and street lights burning that the darkness of evening had indeed descended upon the city. Instead of drowsing, the City of Pleasure was awakening. Out of sheer curiosity, Simple decided to venture out to see this place of pleasure.

Heading across the room, he opened the bedroom door and peered out into the hallway. Seeing no one, he tiptoed quietly down the stairs that circled the large tree.

At the bottom, he cautiously picked up his pace until he reached the large entryway, where he opened the large wooden door and headed out.

It seemed that the city had been transformed with nightfall. The streets were lit up with oil-powered lamps that cast a mysterious dancing glow all around. Dark shadows danced on each sign that hung outside places of business, drawing attention to the activities within. Drinking, gambling, shopping, or any type of show you could imagine could be found within each of these establishments. In the streets themselves, there were many outdoor vendors selling all kinds of wares from clothes to jewelry. At one of these wheeled booths, Simple saw a golden necklace that sparkled as he looked at it. He gazed at the red rubies that lined its neck as well as the goose egg-sized treasure hanging from the end. Not understanding why he was drawn to it, Simple reached his hand into his pocket before remembering that he had no money at all.

Moving on, Simple was drawn in to all that was happening; the bright lights, the sounds of music and dancing. The sour smells of Temporary Satisfaction being served in abundance were everywhere. Walking down the center of the street, Simple looked to his right through an open door on one side of the street and saw several larger groups of people sitting at wooden tables. In their hands were cards, and on the tables were piles of money. Maids and tavern keepers practically danced back and forth across the room, pitchers sloshing as they kept their patrons' glasses full. They yelled encouragements to players who exhibited the first twinges of discouragement on their brows when they lost and patted the backs of the winners, pushing them all on and on towards revelry.

Simple turned, and looking to his left, saw through a different doorway smaller knots of twos playing stones.

At the sound of dice tumbling, he turned and saw other clusters of folks gambling in dark corners between businesses, noting that they were the most raucous of all. Dancing ladies walked the streets, grabbing men and drawing them into the closest establishment. Others rushed by, going from one scene to the next as if they were afraid of missing the next big thing.

In the midst of all this activity, Simple began to notice dark undertones of voices, whispers spoken in the dark places that grabbed at his attention. At first, Simple couldn't tell what the whispers were saying, only that they were there. As he continued on down the street, the whispers got louder. Groups of individuals huddled together and muttered to each other. As Simple passed by he saw the looks of concern in their eyes. Leaning towards one of the groups, he listened more intently and began to get a picture of what they were saying.

It seemed that there was a story that was being told:

"Did you hear? The end is coming. Did you hear? The end is coming!"

The story being shared with urgent whispers was that the City of Pleasure's End was coming soon. Other whispers reached out of the dark, stating that the ending was near for not only the City of Pleasure, but for all of the Old Country. Also, that the time was coming when the borders between Old Country and New Country would be closed for good.

"Get out, get out!" The whispers seemed to say.

Simple saw a larger group gathered on the edge of an alley, and leaning in, heard the final part of the story: that there would be no more crossing over from the Old into the New when the end came. Not only that, but that the Old Country would be destroyed in a hail of fire and brimstone.

This feeling, this sense that they were running out of time, seemed to grow and grow as the group all scattered in every direction. The whispers that were now almost shrieks continued to increase in their intensity. As they they did so, the men and women walking the streets moved more and more frantically about their activities as though in desperate hopes of drowning out their fears of the end. In the taverns, patrons drank more Temporary Satisfaction. Dancers on the streets danced faster. Stakes for gambling grew larger and larger as voices got louder and more raucous in a passionate attempt to drown out the whispers.

Simple stood there in the middle of the road as everything reached an obscene fervor. Worried that the stories he was hearing might be true, Simple conceded to the desperation in the air and began asking the way to the Border. Though no-one seemed to know for sure, each one could point in the same general direction to which Simple began to run with a growing unease and concern in his heart. As he ran across one street and down the next, the shadows cast from tall buildings grew thicker while the lights inviting people to take part in the revelries of the night grew brighter.

He broke free from the increasing madness at the city gate, passing the gate's sentinels, Simple sprinted back towards the Path of Life. A thick fog had descended here outside the gates, making it difficult to stay on the path. The lights of the city first dimming, now disappearing behind him, didn't help. Just before total darkness surrounded him, he saw it. Rising out of the mist were figures that first looked like trees, but as he got closer other shapes came into view. He now knew with certainty in his heart that this was the Border.

The Border crossing just ahead was guarded by large guards in tailored dark blue suits. In front of the guards and across the Path of Life, there was a wooden, counter-weighted traffic arm blocking the narrow path. Standing before that barrier was a line of people.

Drawing closer, Simple noted the anxious looks on their faces as each waited in hopeful expectation to cross over. In a cold sweat from the fog, and heart pumping with both adrenaline and relief, Simple joined the back of the line.

There was somber quietness here outside the city that was in stark contrast to the revelry of the City of Pleasure. One by one, each person in the line ahead of Simple stepped forward and spoke with a guard. After each person had a few moments of discussion with one of the two guards of the border, a guard would pull the counter-weight, and the longer traffic arm would raise up. The approved individual would cross over, and the arm would come down again. Finally, after some time, the person in front of Simple crossed over and Simple was the next in line. His heart froze with suspense as he viewed the serious look on the guard's faces. As he stepped forward up to the crossing, a new, third guard appeared and spoke to the guards that were standing there.

Each of the previous guards then took several steps back from the crossing and the new guard stepped forward. The new guard lifted a long speckled ram's horn to his lips, took a deep breath, and began to blow.

A trumpeting, ear-shattering and majestic sound erupted. Simple felt it through every fiber of his being. The mourning sound increased in volume until even the ground began to tremble and shake. Simple was sure that all the world could hear it, and there was something about this note that while majestic, also struck horror in the core of his being.

After an eternity, the note died away. The guard lowered his horn trumpet and declared, "It is finished!"

He turned back to the other guards, put two fingers to his brow, to which they responded in kind. He nodded and strode away. The first guards turned their backs to the crossing and also strode away into the New Country, leaving the Old Country behind. The dark sky grew even darker, and Simple felt a piercingly cold wind blow as he realized that the rumours had been true.

Now had come the day. The Border Crossing was being permanently shut down. As the darkness grew thicker, he looked back and saw fire and smoke in the distance coming from the City of Pleasure.

Unexpectedly, the ground lurched as the ground heaved. This was a massive shaking, much larger than what Simple had experienced in the Tavern of False Fulfillment, back in Ignorance, except this time it seemed the convulsions that ripped the ground were the kind that would end all life.

As cracks appeared in the ground, plumes of pressurized gases and smoke shot out of those fissures, and Simple smelled the acrid scent of sulfur in the air. It was true; it was all true. This was indeed the end of all things—not only for him, but also for everyone in the Old Country. If only Simple had moved faster towards crossing over into the New Country while he had still had the chance. Now he would never know what it would have been like to have crossed over into the New. Again the ground heaved, this time launching Simple high into the air. As he hurtled back towards the ground, he covered his head and closed his eyes, bracing for impact.

Just before he hit the ground, Simple sat up so quickly that he almost flew up off his bed. In a cold sweat and with his heart beating out of his chest, he looked around in confusion for a good minute. The rays of sun streaming in through the window pierced the clouded haze in Simple's head, and he finally realized it was morning time.

The whole traumatic experience had just been a dream?

Yes?…Yes! It actually had been just a dream!

Hopping out of bed, Simple rushed out the door, practically running down the winding staircase around the magnificent tree that grew from the ground up through the roof. In the mad dash down the stairs, Simple noticed for the first time that there was more than one kind of fruit growing on the tree in addition to its large, beautiful leaves. He almost stopped when he saw a young girl holding a woven basket and perched on a large branch, realizing that it was Insight. She had that mischievous smile on her face, looking down from where she had been picking fruit. At the base of the stairs, Understanding stood with another woven basket of fruit that Insight had passed down. Still feeling the urgency in his heart, Simple simply lifted two fingers to his brow in salute to them and headed on past the sitting room and out the front door of Wisdom's house and out into the city streets.

All of the lights from the lanterns had been replaced with the natural light of a new day. The dancing girls, the sales carts, and the hustle and bustle of the city nightlife were all gone like a morning mist that disappears with the heat of a noonday sun. Simple briskly followed the path he remembered from the dream of the night before, not remembering so much a turn here or turn there as much as general sense of the right direction.

After a short while, he heard a racket just up ahead and looked over, realizing he was in front of the house that he had passed the day before with Wisdom. It was the house of the Adulteress.

The ruckus coming from the house was clearly the sounds of something being thrown and of those thrown items crashing into other things inside. Suddenly, broken glass exploded the quietness of the early morning and a young man came flying out the door backwards and fell into a heap at the bottom of the steps. This was the same young man that had been drawn into the house by Adulteress the night before. Charging out of the doors after the young man came an older man with a bow in one hand and an arrow in the other.

It became obvious by what followed that this second man was the husband of the Adulteress that had been assumed to be gone till the next full moon. Overcome with fear, the young man quickly got up to his feet. He backpedaled, pleading, "I'll give you anything! Anything you ask for, I'll get it for you! Just please don't kill me!"

"You think to bribe me?" The husband scoffed. "Here you are with the one that I love, and you think I'll take money? I'll tell you just what I'm willing to take. I'll take your life, that's exactly what I'll take! Believe me when I say that this arrow will pierce your liver this day!" The husband lifted his bow, fitted the arrow, and drew it taut, aiming at the young fool.

Having not been paying attention to where he was going, the young man backed up even faster into a waist-high pillar on the top of which sat a brazier full of the hot coals that had taken the edge off the night's chill. The bowl of coals fell off the column, dumping the whole mass of coals all around, particularly right into the young man's lap as he turned. Screaming in pain, the young man screeched and flailed as he was burned. Those screams took on a whole new tenor when he began stepping on the coals that were now scattered on every side. Falling on the ground, he continued to push himself back away from the enraged husband who now had the arrow drawn up alongside his cheek, just under his right ear.

Simple heard the twang of a bow's string and a thud followed by a yelp, which ended as quick as it sounded. Simple turned and ran, horrified at what was happening.

In terror, he tore down the street and turned one corner, another corner, then the next. After a little distance had been placed between himself and the Adulteress' house, Simple slowed down just enough to look back. It was at that moment, at the place where two streets came together, he plowed into a large, overweight man. Drawing up to a stop, Simple regarded the large man he had just collided with and saw that he had a black stovetop hat and full-length cloak the color of night.

"I dare say, young man, you're off in quite a hurry. Where are you headed in such fashion?" said the man.

"I'm sorry, sir. My name is Simple, and I just saw the most horrific deed back at the house of the Adulteress."

"Well, I'd think that anyone who doesn't know better than to spend any amount of time at all with that trollop deserves whatever they get. I'll hear no more about the likes of her. Let me introduce myself, young man. My name is Mr. Intellectual and it's a pleasure to meet you, Simple. We both seem to be headed the same way, and it's a beautiful day, why don't we walk a talk awhile."

"Sounds good to me," Simple replied as they both continued down the street.

"Tell me, young Simple, where are you off to today?"

"Well, to be honest," Simple said reluctantly, "Last night I dreamed that I was walking the streets of the City of Pleasure. In that dream, I heard rumors that the Old Country was going to be destroyed in fire and brimstone, and the only way to avoid it was to cross over from the Old Country to the New Country. This dream seemed to bring such insight that I believe it's true. I'm now off to see the guards at the Border Crossing so I can cross from the Old Country into the New Country before the end of all things here in the Old Country."

"Well isn't that just fascinating," said Mr. Intellectual in a sarcastic voice. "It looks like you've just gotten out of bed, so it's obvious you're not thinking clearly. Let me tell you exactly what I think. I believe dreams are not worth listening to. In fact, in my opinion, dreams can be one of the dangerous consequences of drinking Pure Delight. You know if you take the time to really think about it and process this information, you would see clearly as I do that these rumors of the Old Country burning or disappearing can't possibly be true. Have you ever heard of something like that happening before? No, of course, you haven't, and that's why it will never happen, and you should put off this foolishness and go enjoy a glass of Temporary Satisfaction."

Simple looked up as he heard crows cawing in the distance. He then turned to Mr. Intellectual and said, "I've had Temporary Satisfaction, and believe me, I know that it's just temporary. I've been traveling the Path of Life looking for something a little more real than temporary pleasures."

"Hmmm," said Mr. Intellectual. "I can't change the mind of a man who's had his own experience. What is it you think to accomplish, traveling the Path of Life?"

"Well," replied Simple thoughtfully as he walked along, "To meet the King is why I'm taking this trip. I was living in Ignorance on Dead End Lane, and Sower of Seed shared with me news of the King. At that time, a seed was sown in my heart and so here I am traveling on this journey to find the King."

"Have you ever met this King?"

"No," Simple replied, again lowering and shaking his head.

"Off to meet a King you've never seen? That just doesn't make any sense to me!"

They continued down the road around one last bend and out the gates of the City of Pleasure, and then Simple saw something that made him exclaim: "I knew it! There are the guards of my dream!"

"My boy, I've no idea what you're talking about," Mr. Intellectual said. "That there's the path to what I hear is the most distressing part of the country and all I see standing there are a few guards in blue suits looking out for riffraff like you to throw in jail! I can't believe I've wasted my time with you."

Mr. Intellectual turned away from Simple and with a huff and a puff headed back into the City of Pleasure. Simple lifted two fingers to the brow, then turned towards the Border Crossing.

Venturing out in the City of Pleasure at night

7

BORDER CROSSING

No-one can enter the New Country
unless they are born of water and the Spirit...you must
confess with your mouth and believe with your heart
and you will be saved.

I t was a marvelously beautiful day. The shining sun
was about to crest the top of the trees in the
distance and in front of the forest wound a gentle
river with crystal-clear waters. A fish leaped in the
distance as the water babbled around stones close to the
shore. Simple took a deep breath as he left the City of
Pleasure behind and, with anticipation and some
urgency, tread down the Path of Life that ended at the
border crossing between the Old Country and the New
Country.

A counter-weighted red and white traffic arm stood
blocking the Path of Life, and behind it stood two

watchmen in tailored blue cloaks keeping vigil over the crossing. They watched Simple draw near. Simple was concerned, thinking about Mr. Intellectual's comment that they might think him a riffraff looking to cause trouble. Instead, as Simple looked into their eyes, he saw a gentleness that complemented their tough strength.

Arriving at the arm, Simple lowered his head, not knowing what to say or do. The first guard looked Simple over with a solemn gaze and said in a loud, clear voice, "Do you wish to cross over from that which is Old, and into the New?"

"I do," Simple whispered.

"Do you recognize the reign of the King in all of the land, both of the Old Country as well as the New?"

Simple looked up, meeting the guard's gaze, eye to eye.

"Sir, I've never met this King you speak of. I first heard of him from Sower of Seed. Others like Faith, Good Samaritan and Wisdom all claim to be part of his Kingdom, while others like Wasted Time and Folly swear he doesn't exist. It seems that some don't believe in him at all, while those that say they've met him say he's the best. Though I've never met him, I want to believe. If what I've heard is really true, then yes, I believe."

"Blessed are those who believe, but have never seen," the guard said. "Step forward."

The white and red crossbar that separated Simple from the guard rose, and Simple crossed over from the Old Country into the New Country.

At that moment, it was as though Simple was seeing through new eyes. He had stepped from black and white to color; from death to life. The radiance of the green grass, the rough, brown bark on the trees, and many-colored flowers struck him with their beauty. Butterflies and dragonflies danced while bees buzzed from one place to the next.

The first guard stepped to the side while the second motioned with his hand to follow him. He led Simple on down the Path of Life till they reached the gentle river. There, at the river's edge, they stepped in and waded out through the clear waters till they reached the middle, and the water was just almost chest deep. The guard then stopped and turned back towards Simple. Very solemnly, like the first guard, he said to Simple, "You have entered into the River of Life. Any who would truly live must pass through the waters and experience rebirth. Simple, you must choose this day whom you will serve. Do you accept the King of all the lands as your Lord and Master?"

"I do."

"Are you willing to be the King's servant from this day forward and follow him wherever he may lead?"

"I will."

The guard then put his left hand on the back of Simple's head and his right palm over Simple's mouth with nose gently squeezed between the nook of thumb and forefinger and said "My fellow servant, I baptize you in the name of the King of all the Kingdom." The guard then declared with a loud voice, "Out with the old and in with the new!"

Leaning Simple backwards into the water and submerging him until he was fully immersed, the guard then lifted him back up joyfully declaring. "Death is swallowed up by life!"

Rising up out of the water, Simple blinked as the water poured down out of his hair and over his face.

An eruption of yelling and clapping then occurred on the side of the river he had just come from. Looking back, he saw many people hooting and hollering, shouting encouragements while laughing and clapping their hands. Upon closer scrutiny, he noticed Wisdom, Discernment, Understanding, and Insight as well as the Good Samaritan included in the crowd, all beaming.

"Way to go, Simple!" yelled the Good Samaritan.

"You chose wisely!" Wisdom cried out.

"Way to follow your dream!" laughed Insight.

"We knew you'd make the right choice!" Discernment called out.

As his vision continued to clear, Simple saw a lone white dove glide down off a nearby oak tree to land on a log near the water's edge. The dove looked towards Simple with a gaze of innocence.

What a stark contrast to the black flock of Stealers of Seed, Simple thought.

At that moment, Simple felt the seed that had been planted in his heart by Sower of Seed explode into life as its petals opened in Simple's heart. The seed that had been planted so long ago, while forgotten to Simple's conscious mind, had never disappeared. Where there had been the initial pain of change as the seed had burrowed itself down in his heart, that pain had become so familiar that it was almost unnoticeable. Now that life had sprung from the dead seed, he was aware of how much pain he'd carried and was thankful for the unburdening as the wonderful lightness of joy took its place.

After a short while of enjoying the moment and the cheers, Simple allowed the guard to lead him on across the River of Life. The well-wishers shouted encouragements for the rest of Simple's journey across the river as they waved their farewells and then headed back towards the Old Country.

"Have a rest here," said the guard.

Simple sat down on a log, letting the sun and crisp air start to dry his clothes and body.

"You've had quite the journey and have done well to get here," the guard said. "We never quite know when the crossing will be closed for good."

"So I'm not completely bonkers then!" Simple said with relief. "I wasn't quite sure if a dream I had last night was insight into mysteries of the Kingdom or if those "mysteries" were just fantasies." He combed his wet hair with his fingers and smiled, grateful for the information he was getting. "What do you know of the timing when these borders will be closed for good?"

"Truthfully, we don't know. What we do know is that the King could send the order for the permanent closing at any time. We must live each day, faithful to what we're called to do, not knowing if it will be our last. It's our desire that as many cross over as possible before the end comes. So there have been many ambassadors of the King hard at work, often in difficult environments. There are many, including those of Folly's extended family that work actively to oppose the crossing over of pilgrims from the Old Country to the New."

"Thanks so much," Simple said, sincerely. "Will you be going with me on the Path of Life to show me where I should go from here?"

The guard laughed as he looked towards the trees and said, "No, I won't. Those that know Faith have no need of a guard to go with them on the Path of Life. It's been my pleasure, Simple," he said with a smile. "Best of luck to you on your journey." He put two fingers to the brow, turned, and headed back across the River of Life.

Even as the guard strode away, Simple noticed movement from the forest behind him and turned to see another man striding his way, face beaming with joy.

"Faith!" Simple exclaimed.

As Simple watched Faith coming his way, he noticed that Faith seemed older, healthier, and stronger than any of the times he had seen him before. His face had a glow that simply radiated and caused Simple to smile.

"Hi there, Simple!" Faith said as he walked up. "I'm so glad that your journey has brought you into the New Country, and across the River of Life. I was confident that you would make it, even when we first met in Ignorance and the Stealers of Seed tried to stop your journey before it had even started! I must admit, I was a little concerned when you took up with Deceitfulness of Wealth, but thankfully you didn't meet the end that he intended for you. Others have not been so lucky."

"Yeah, Deceitfulness of Wealth really got me when he talked about needing to have money to eat and to lodge when I got to the City of Pleasure. I should've trusted that if I stayed on the Path of Life, that the King would see me through. Thankfully, Wisdom was at the path along the way by the gates into the city and took good care of me. Speaking of Wisdom and her family, I wonder who those others were that cheering with them."

"Those were also members of Wisdom's family, the same family you are now a member of as well." Faith said. "They are the ones that have traveled the Path of Life, become citizens of the New Country and have met the King. Under the King's instructions, they now cross back into the Old Country to help free others from the lies and manipulations of Wasted Time and his family and encourage them to cross over from the old to the new before it's too late."

Out of the blue, Simple's eyelids became very heavy and he yawned.

Seeing this, Faith said, "Why don't you lie down for a little while and rest? I'm sure we'll be talking together again real soon."

And just like that, Faith was gone again. Yet, somehow, Simple had no doubt he was close at hand.

Peacefully tired, Simple, lay down on the lush green grass near the riverbank, using the log the dove had rested on as a headrest. He gazed out at the clear waters of the flowing river. The witnesses to the crossing were gone. The guards were gone. It was so peaceful, so quiet, especially compared to the loud raucousness of the City of Pleasure. Simple took a deep breath of fresh air, enjoying the earthiness of the ground and sense of growing life he could feel all around. He nodded off to sleep just as the dove returned and settled on his shoulder.

He dreamed…

Simple was sitting on the log by the River of Life when the King stepped out from the same woods that Faith had come from. In appearance he was a man, a kind-looking man, but clearly a man of authority, very regal and kingly in his own special sort of way.

The King walked towards Simple, and the smile on his face communicated more than words could describe: love, compassion, concern, but mixed with joy, elation and a euphoric happiness. The King was wearing a noble and resplendent white robe embroidered with many colors and precious stones. The train of this magnificent garment was hemmed in gold thread and it trailed behind him.

Walking up to Simple, the King sat next to him on the log and in a fatherly tone, began to speak.

"Welcome to the New Country, Simple! I'm so glad you're here. Thank you for paying attention to Sower of Seed. The shakings in the Town of Ignorance certainly prepared the way for him to sow seed, not only in your heart, but the hearts of many others as well.

I know the journey is tough, but you've done well to leave Ignorance behind and travel the Path of Life.

Though you couldn't see Me, I have been with you and spoken with you all along your journey on the Path of Life. From here, the journey on the Path of Life continues and is still fraught with trials and difficulty, but by coming here today you have crossed over from the old way of journeying into new ways of traveling. You made a decision to seek Me and you have found Me and will eternally find Me more and more."

The King stood up and walked over to the waters of the River of Life and knelt down. He scooped a handful of gravel from the river's edge and returned. Sitting down again, he lifted his cupped hands together with palms upraised and held them out to Simple "Look into my hands. What do you see, Simple?"

Looking closely, Simple replied, "I see many stones."

"That is correct. Look closer. What do you see?"

Leaning over, Simple peered closer into the King's hands, studied the stones, and saw a little sparkle of red as the sun hit it just right.

"Wait. Is that a ruby in the midst of the stones?" As Simple continued inspecting the stones, he noticed sparkles of white, then green. "I see a diamond and an emerald!"

"You have seen rightly. All along your journey, you will find that there are treasures hidden in the midst of what looks to be common, everyday stones, even worthless-looking stones. Every conversation you have, every dream you have in the night, even imaginings you have throughout the day are like encountering this handful of stones. Many of those stones have no value, but hidden in the midst of seemingly worthless situations are often incredible treasures. As your King, I adjure you this day, my servant, to be a man that looks for the treasures that are found in the normal outlay of life. And when your journey is over, you'll be surprised at the tremendous treasure you've accumulated."

There are those that spend their lives amassing worthless stones—those like Wasted Time and members of his family. Even others that live in Ignorance. When they come to the end of their life, they will come before me at the great White Throne and will pour out all that they've stored up over their lives. I will put my purifying fire to the mound that is their lives, and when it's consumed, we will all find that their lives were indeed wasted. Those that have paid attention to look for treasure will find that the final fire of purification will leave them with great rewards.

You on the other hand, are not of those of Ignorance any longer, but have crossed over into the New Country and are to look for these treasures. You are being given the opportunity to store up treasures of tremendous worth that have eternal value. They will benefit you not only in the day of the end, the day of new beginnings, but they are to benefit others you encounter along the Path of Life as well. Some of those treasures may not look like much at the time you receive them, but believe me—over time, their value will be made known.

Remember that you've crossed over from the old into the new. New and Old are not geographical boundaries, as you will continue to deal with the attacks from Wasted Time and his family even in the New Country. My Kingdom is not of this world, but is much greater. Remember and do not forget, you are to look for the precious stones!

I'm not leaving you alone, but am giving you a book that will help you to grow in the new. This book will give you guidance as you travel the Path of Life. Read this book daily and contemplate the words. When you think on these things, you will receive treasures that will enrich your life, empower you and position you to help others. You must remember: the words of this book are true no matter how you feel, no matter what others say, no matter what you see. I say it again: The words of this book are true!

Anytime you want to talk with Me, just talk like I'm there with you. Feel free to ask Me anything! You'll be surprised at how much closer we'll seem and how I answer your questions. This journey down the Path of Life is exactly that—a journey. There will be times that are more difficult, and times that are easier, but fear not; I'm with you wherever you go."

The King stood up, then gently ruffling Simple's hair, leaned in and whispered, "I'm with you always."

As a cool breeze ruffled Simple's hair, he felt the warmth of the sun on his face and breathed in the scent of fresh earth, flowers and trees. He opened his eyes, waking from his peaceful dream. He sat up, his back to the log. The white dove that had been perched there as he'd slept cooed, then took to the air in a flutter. It circled the clearing and the river, then winged its way up the Path of Life, into the forest and out of sight. Sitting there in peaceful contemplation, Simple stretched his arms, then noticed a book enclosed in a brown leather cover, right where the dove had been perched. Standing up, he picked up the book and examined the smooth gold leaf illustration on its cover. It was of a large tree with roots below as large and round as the limbs above the trunk. The title above it read: "The Book of Life."

Sitting down on the log, Simple considered yet again the milestones of his journey thus far to enter the New Country. The shakings in the town of Ignorance that had prepared the soil of his heart for the timely Sower of Seed. The meeting of Faith on that first path where Stealers of Seed had tried to turn him back to the Tavern of False Fulfillment. How Faith seemed to grow so quickly on his journey from a small boy with tattered cloak to the ruddy, strong and much wiser man he seemed to be today. While the journey had been hard, Simple felt thankful for every part of it, because it felt that for some reason, it was preparation for what was coming ahead.

The King had been clear: Wasted Time and his family's attacks would not disappear now that he had crossed over. However, he did have this Book of Life to help him on his journey. So, Simple opened the book and slowly began to read.

**The King teaches Simple to search for
treasures in the midst of worthless stones**

8

GIFT BRINGER

Foolish things shame the wise.

The next morning, Simple awoke from a pleasant night's sleep under the stars. He got up, stretched and noticing he was thirsty, bent down and drank from the crisp, clear and refreshing waters of the River of Life. The water was as good as expected, reminding him strongly of the Pure Delight that Wisdom had shared with him.

Returning to the log by the side of the river, Simple sat and wondered about what his journey would look like now that he was in the New Country. Remembering that the King had told him that the Book of Life would give him daily guidance, Simple picked up the book and began to read. After he read for awhile, a particular passage stood out to him. In fact, it almost seemed to glow. Simple focused on that section and pondered the words: "Foolish things shame the wise." Not knowing the meaning, but feeling like it was somehow important, Simple filed those words away in his mind to meditate and think on during his journey today.

Feeling it was time to get up and get going, Simple put the book into a single-strapped leather pouch that he had found on the other end of the log. He strung the weathered leather strap over his head and onto his shoulder where the pouch could hang from the opposite side of his waist. Standing up, Simple began walking once again down the continuation of the Path of Life and headed into the woods in the same direction the dove had flown.

Excited about what he would find in the New Country, Simple continued on the path through the woods, thinking about everything the King had said in his dream. He continued pondering the words he had read: *Foolish things shame the wise.*

Leaving Ignorance always seemed foolish to me until the shakings woke me up, Simple thought to himself. *Always thought it was the smart thing to do, drinking Temporary Satisfaction and boy, Wasted Time had me fooled into believing there was nothing better. But I wonder what foolish things of the Kingdom are so powerful that they shame the wise.*

While walking the Path of Life, Simple spotted up ahead a man, the most interesting-looking man sitting on a rock on the side of the path. With his legs crossed and eyes closed, the man sat on the top of a gray, white rock that was about waist high. As Simple walked closer, he realized that the man's lips were moving and from his mouth were coming downright weird sounds. The sounds, quite frankly, sounded like gibberish, but the man spoke it continually like he was fluent in a language Simple had never heard before. Coming to a stop in front of the man, he considered how foolish this man sounded. After thinking about whether to keep walking or wait,

Simple recognized the familiar and confident like peace that the man exuded that had seemed to characterize the King's ambassadors. In hopes that this was in fact another of the King's men, he waited and prepared himself for what this one might have to share.

After an awkward wait, Simple decided to go ahead and speak up.

"What are you doing?" Simple asked quietly, not wanting to disturb the man, but excited to begin a conversation.

The man jerked slightly as though taken by surprise and abruptly closed his mouth. Then opening one eye, he looked Simple over, then shut his eye again. He tilted his head, then after seemingly to think about it a moment longer, he opened his eyes and said, "Well, hello there! I'm Gift Bringer, one of the King's Ambassadors, what's your name?"

"I'm Simple."

"I thought that might be you. I've been sent to bring you a gift that will help you on the rest of your journey down the Path of Life. A gift I'm excited to share with you. Have a seat here on this rock right next to me. I have some things I'd like to share with you regarding your journey now that you're here in the New Country."

Simple sat on the top of the rock and made himself comfortable.

Gift Bringer continued: "You, Simple, are made of three main parts: your mind, body, and spirit. Throughout your journey, you've used your mind to process the world around you and make decisions, as well as your physical body to act on those decisions. Unfortunately, your mind's been filled with strongholds of ways of thinking that were put there by life in Ignorance and instigated by Wasted Time and his family.

The shakings in the town of Ignorance shook the hold those strongholds had on you, waking you up to the ideas and feelings that something wasn't right. As you've physically travelled the Path of Life, your journey has been as much of a process of overcoming wrong ways of thinking as much as it has been a physical journey.

However, when you passed through the gate at the border crossing and were immersed into the waters of the River of Life, your spirit was awakened—reborn, if you will. Now you must feed your newborn spirit with the milk of the Word of Life. What a wonderful exercise for you, because you'll find that as you're spiritually nourished by the milk of the words of the Book of Life, those words will also become a sword that is powerful for demolishing the strongholds that have been set up in your mind against the knowledge of the King. You'll continue to grow in experience and maturity of this as you feast on the reading of the Words of Life daily.

Those that enter by the gate into the New Country must continually feed not only their bodies, but their spirits in this way if they're going to overcome the traps of Wasted Time and his family. Although you are in the New Country, there are usurpers who have not entered correctly by the gate and lay traps along the way to distract and keep you from pursuing your journey on the Path of Life.

You've received the Words of Life from the King. Read it daily—this is important! In addition to sharing all that with you, I've been sent here by the King to share with you a new language of the Kingdom that will increase your ability to receive from the Words of Life. It's a spiritual gift, a faith language that allows you to speak mysteries with your spirit!

And that's what I've been doing here on the side of the road, speaking mysteries with my spirit! What do you think about that?"

Not knowing what he thought about it, Simple said, " I don't know. I'm sorry Gift Bringer, but what mysteries are you speaking?"

"Well, quite frankly—I don't know yet," he replied, to Simple's surprise.

Gift Bringer straightened his legs and hopped down off the rock, brushing off some leaves and grass from the back of his legs. Then putting a hand on Simple's shoulder, he said with a big smile: "Knowing what mysteries I'm speaking—that part just usually comes later!

When you speak in a spiritual language, those things that you speak by faith are in fact mysteries that have been hidden in secret places. You are speaking to the King mysteries through the words you speak and by doing this, you conscientiously bypass your conscious understanding and release mysteries that are hidden by faith. When you exercise this gift in that way, the gift is so powerful, it charges up your spirit like a battery. When your spirit is charged up, then over time these mysteries that you're speaking cross over from hiddenness to understanding and thus to outward manifestation.

Like I said, the faith act of speaking in a spiritual language feeds your spirit in such a way that it releases power to your spirit like a battery charging you up until revelation is activated and those hidden mysteries switch over from hiddenness into a place of insight and understanding. And believe me, when we travel the Path of Life, we need all the insight and understanding we can get!" Gift Bringer said, chuckling. Then his face turned serious as he looked at Simple. "Would you like a spiritual language too?"

"What you've described sounds good, but I don't know," Simple stammered and became red in the face. After a moment shifting his feet back and forth and looking around, he finally looked Gift Bringer in the eye and explained: "You sound awfully silly."

"I know, right?" Gift Bringer retorted. "Foolish things have a way of turning out to be better than you can believe!"

"Well, if one does receive this gift of a spiritual language, how often should someone speak in their spiritual language?" Simple asked.

"The King has decreed that each person shall practice their gifts in accordance with the measure of their faith. Generally, the more one knows the person of Faith, the more one tends to exercise their King-given gifts. Spiritual gifts like one's spiritual language are not a measure of value or of importance in the Kingdom, because only the King knows how much each person has been given. However, it does feed your spirit and you will grow stronger in revelatory understanding of the Kingdom and increase in maturity, "

"Since I don't know this language that you're speaking of, how would I start?"

"Well, Simple, it's different for everybody. Some folks, when they're ready to begin, wait for the gift in a moment of quiet and then experience something like lightning or electricity flow through them, and then out comes a spontaneous burst of sound! However, most people simply open their mouth and make sounds that feel right in faith and realize over time that their act of faith has borne great fruit. Either way of learning is neither right nor wrong, what matters is that it's life giving and brings peace and joy."

"Once you start talking in your language, what happens?" Simple asked, scratching his head.

"There are many benefits! Freedom from the fear of what others think is a good one and this releases more power in our lives than you'd expect. Like I said before, it's also like being plugged into a power source and getting your spiritual battery charged up. One of the benefits I like most is that when you speak in the Spirit, it's a form of communication with the King. One's mind seems unfruitful because they're uttering mysteries with their Spirit. But those mysteries start to take substance and somehow, someway, we experience an outward manifestation of inward promise as we receive greater revelation from the King. Now, this is only one of many gifts that the King gives, so don't get too hung up on it. But should you choose to receive it, then enjoy it, because it sure is great!"

"Do I have to receive it and do it?"

"Do you have to do it? No, of course not. It's a free gift from the King! Like I said, Simple, it simply increases your capacity to understand and receive more from the King. It's like eating healthy and exercising; some choose to do it and some don't, but the ones that do eat healthy and exercise tend to be stronger, have more energy, can go longer, live longer and generally have happier lives. The ones that don't, don't. Only the ones that do choose to use their gift experience the good effects that come from it. Of course, we don't understand it fully; it's one of those mysteries of the King.

People who can't abide mystery in general don't do it; those who can, do. Do you remember the very large Mr. Intellectual from the Old Country who couldn't even grasp that the gate to the border to the New Country was right in front of him?"

Simple nodded his head in recollection. Laughing, Gift Bringer said, "Let's just say he'd have a hard time with what I'm sharing with you now! I tell you what— let's just try it! Open your mouth. Don't worry about anything or anybody else. I promise not to tell anyone! "

After thinking about it a minute, Simple reluctantly agreed. He began making what sounded like some choking noises. Then he paused and both he and Gift

Bringer looked at each other. After the awkward pause, they both burst out laughing!

"Go ahead and try again," Gift Bringer said. "Take your time. I'm not headed anywhere." Adjusting, Simple opened his mouth again, saying something like, "Dadadadadada."

"OK, now move your tongue around. You've got it! There you go!"

"Shadadadad qui, neyokoshay," Simple continued with eyes closed.

"Just keep practicing and you will get better and better."

"I feel foolish," Simple said.

"Of course it feels foolish. Not only that, but you look and sound ridiculous! But, remember how the King wrote the words in the Book of Life: 'Foolish things shame the wise.' It actually is foolish and that's why it feels that way. However, the foolishness of the things of the Spirit are wiser than man's greatest wisdom. When you run into people without a grid for this, pay them no mind! Folks don't like to admit it, but in general they tend to be against just about anything that they don't actually do themselves or don't understand. It takes humility to recognize that one's personal experience is not the extent of what's possible or best!"

"Got it. As I do this, I don't really feel like anything is going on. Am I supposed to feel different, or feel waves of power washing over me?" Simple asked.

"When it's daytime and you flip the switch for a lamp to come on, you may not notice how much, if any light is shining from that lamp. But rest assured, when nighttime comes, and light is needed you'll find that understanding and insight will shine brighter and further than it would of otherwise. You will be very glad in those times of darkness that you have a lamp that shines bright!"

"Well, it's been great talking with you. I hope you enjoy your gift! I've got King's business to attend to, a few more gifts to pass out, so I'm off!" Gift Bringer gave Simple a big smile and a squeeze on the shoulder, then walked on down the Path of Life. After heading down a ways, he turned and hollered back one last admonition, "Don't forget to practice!" With two fingers to the brow, Gift Bringer turned back and soon he was gone from sight.

"They say there's no time like the present," Simple said out loud. He sat cross-legged on the large rock by the roadside, closed his eyes and began to practice. "Dadadadadadodedadai...."

After some time, Simple heard someone say, "Excuse me, but what are you saying?"

Simple opened his eyes to find a man wearing a white gown with two wooden sticks tied together crossways hanging by a leather strap around his neck standing in front of him.

"Oh," Simple said sheepishly. "Just practicing my spiritual language."

"What? A spiritual language?" The man picked up the large wooden cross that hung from around his chest with his left hand, pointed it at Simple and then began making the signs of the cross with his right hand over and over. "Are you mad? Are you simply insane? That's crazy, I tell you! I've heard of this thing before and it's foolishness and a complete waste of time. How in the name of the King of all the Kingdom could random sounds coming out of your mouth do anybody any good?" the man asked.

"To be frank, I don't know," Simple said with a shrug. "All I know is that this journey on the Path of Life in the New Country seems to be different than the journey as it was in the Old Country and I'm looking to learn everything I can. The King spoke to me in a dream when I crossed the border and he adjured me to look for treasures in the midst of worthless stones. While I don't know yet if this thing is a treasure or worthless stone, I think it's worth finding out!"

"You were in the Old Country?" the man stammered.

"Yes, just yesterday. That's when I spoke with the King."

"You spoke to the King? Now I know you're not just foolish, but completely crazy. You are on the Path of Lies!"

The man ended his sentence with a vehement scream. He then began backing away from Simple, making more symbols with his hands, then finally kissed his wooden object and ran like fire was licking at his feet. As he ran down the path, the gown tangled up into his feet and the man tripped, launching spreadeagled on the ground and hitting his head on a rock on the side of the path. Dazed and confused for a moment, the man sat up nursing the wound on his head. Noticing that the front of his cloak was red, the man took off the leather strap, as the two sticks had broken when he'd landed on them. Simple now saw that they had pierced his chest.

Struggling to his feet, the man straightened himself and stood there shakily till he looked back and saw Simple still sitting there on the rock looking at him. The man glanced down at his chest, pulled the sticks off and threw them down. Then the man screamed, "No! This is the Path of Lies, the Path of Lies!" At that point, the man ran off the Path of Life and into the forest.

Simple gaped as the ridiculousness of that man, then thought to himself: *I wonder if that man will ever be seen again? I don't know anything about that man, but I do know this: the King has been good to me and I trust him. The ambassadors that have come my way have been very helpful and I think I'm going to keep on, keeping on, rather than worry about what some weird stranger I've never met thinks about it, thank you very much.*

Then, Simple stood up and continued down the Path of Life, eager for the adventures that lay ahead.

The Book of Life

9

SPIRITUAL BLINDNESS

If any two will agree in my name,
then I will do what they request.

The next morning, Simple rose early, excited about the day's adventures. Soon, he was walking down the Path of Life. The sun was shining while a cool breeze fluttered green leaves on their branches throughout the forest. It was the perfect weather for walking. As he hiked down the Path of Life, Simple meditated to himself with his new spiritual language, trying out different sounds to see how they felt on his tongue: "Dadadadade. Dadadadado Dadadadadu."

You know, once you got past the initial weirdness and took the time to think about it, it was actually kind of fun. Making this type of meditation exercise a focal point of his attention really seemed to center his thoughts. The result was a pivoting in his spirit from the past tension of the journey to a clarity of mind while traveling that he'd not realized was missing before. He could now hear sounds of the limbs of the trees moving as the wind blew, the birds chirping and the occasional coo of a dove. This experience of the quiet of nature around him while he was meditating resulted in a release of anxiety and stress. This was now a peaceful walk through the forest on a wonderful day rather than an uncertain venture into the unknown.

It was so perfect that Simple decided to stop and take a break to read the Book of Life as the King had encouraged him to do. So, he sat on a right-sized stone at one side of the Path of Life and positioned himself comfortably. Taking the Book of Life out of the leather pouch, he took the time to caress and enjoy the gold-embossed Tree of Life on the front. Opening the book to where he had left off the day before, he began to read. As Simple read, he took the time to consider and process in his thinking the things he read. Not really sure of what he was expecting to happen, Simple remembered the King's instruction to look for hidden treasures. This idea spiked a renewed interest in what he was reading, and the further he read, it was as though the plant in his heart that had been born was being watered and strengthened into a young tree. After awhile, he read a passage that almost began to glow. He paused, reread that passage and then considered. *If any two will agree in my name, then I will do what they request.*

Here was a treasure, he just knew it! It was like finding a jewel on the ground and knowing it was valuable, but not knowing its full worth. In the same way, he felt a kind of sparkle from the passage that had caught his spirit's eye. Yet, until it worked its way out in his everyday life, he wasn't quite sure what the application would be. If today was anything like yesterday, when Bringer of Gifts had brought the outward manifestation of the hidden truth that "foolish things shame the wise" through his new spiritual language, then perhaps he'd find out what this meant as he continued his journey on the Path of Life. Simple closed the book, and then took a few more minutes to meditate in quiet. After a while, he put the book back into his pouch, strapped it on and returned to traveling the Path of Life.

As Simple journeyed on the Path of Life, the scenery began to change. Though there were still trees on both sides of the path, the left side of the path began to angle and drop off downwards just past the first trees to a significant ditch on that side of the road. Steadying himself against a tree on that side of the Path, Simple leaned out over the ditch and saw bright green lichen growing on the rocks below. He also saw that it would be difficult to climb out of that ditch if one by chance fell in, so he moved over towards the right side of the Path of Life and continued.

Later in the day, when the sun was at its peak, Simple saw the silhouette of a person in the distance. As he approached about a stone's throw away from the fellow traveler, he saw that it was another man walking the path just as he was. Yet, something seemed kind of strange, odd and somehow familiar about the man as he shuffled slowly along the left side of the road. Once he was within spitting distance of the man, Simple saw that the man, a lanky fellow, was walking into a low branch that hung over the side of the Path of Life. As the man walked forward, the branch would hit him in the head. He'd then back up, turn a little and then walk into the same branch, over and over again. Because the ground angled down towards the ditch on that side of the path, no matter which way the man turned, he just didn't seem to turn the right way as the incline steered him away from the road and towards the ditch. Thankfully, the branch was stopping him from going straight into the ditch.

As he neared arm's length from the man, Simple saw by the man's graying hair that he was a bit older then he was. He also noticed that the man had some kind of strange scales on his face. Where the man's eyes should have been there was what appeared to be a thick webbing that covered them. It was clear that the man couldn't see anything at all and was in need of help. Just then, the man managed to push his way past the branch and stepped onto the downward slope heading right towards the ditch.

Simple leaped forward, grabbing the man by his upper arm and yelled, "Wait! You're heading off the road into a ditch."

Startled, the man jumped briefly, then slowly stepped backwards as Simple guided him onto the Path of Life again. Speaking up, Simple said, "I'm sorry sir, I couldn't help but notice that you look like you could use some help. There's a deep ditch on that side of the Path of Life and a low-hanging branch on the last tree that was holding you back from falling."

The man cocked his head in the direction of Simple. "Ditch?" he exclaimed. "I had no idea. Thank you very much, kind sir, for your help."

"Well, I did notice from quite a ways back as I was walking that you have seemed to be at an impasse for awhile," Simple replied. "Did you know that you were walking into the branch of a tree? You kept turning this way and that way, but each time you moved forward, you kept walking into the same tree branch. You're not really on the Path of Life at all, just kind of on the side of it."

"Is that right?" exclaimed the man with excitement. "Faith had told me that those who call on the King will be saved. Here I was, feeling like I wasn't going anywhere. I had just prayed to the King just as if He were right here with me to show me where to go. I thought I had a breakthrough, but with the momentum I was feeling from going down the incline, I knew I was falling forward out of control. Then out of the blue, here you are saving the day for me and telling me what I need to hear! Thank you so much for your assistance!"

"Absolutely, so glad I happened to be here," Simple replied.

"My name is Hunger," the man said. "It wasn't too many days back when I met Sower of Seed back in Ignorance and I decided to travel the Path of Life and look for the King. A kind man named Faith has been with me often on this journey, just seeming to show up right when I need him—kind of like what happened when you arrived just now. Faith said if I looked for the King earnestly I would find him. Don't know if I'm getting anywhere, but if what I heard about the King is true, I'm trusting he will find me and direct me in the way I should go."

Taking Hunger by the arm, Simple said, "Well, it's very nice to meet you, Hunger. Here, let me direct you back onto the Path of Life." Simple took Hunger's hand and placed it on his shoulder and together they walked around the tree branch and situated themselves on the Path of Life in the direction they were both headed. "Since we're both headed the same way, why don't you walk with me awhile? I'd appreciate the company."

"Well thank you again. It'd be a pleasure to walk with a fellow pilgrim." And with Hunger's right hand on Simple's left shoulder, they continued walking down the road.

"If you don't mind my asking, what are those scales over your eyes?" asked Simple. "They look like the reason you can't see or stay on the Path of Life."

"Once upon a time, I lived back in the Old Country in the village of Ignorance. Had a place over on the Boulevard of Broken Dreams. Things were so hard up for me that I would travel down Dead End Lane and frequent the Tavern of False Fulfillment. I spent so much time drinking Temporary Satisfaction that I built up a tab with Wasted Time that I could never pay back. At first, he let me work some of it off, doing some cleaning here and there. After quite awhile, the satisfaction of the drink wasn't even temporary, so I moved to the harder stuff and began taking shots of Lost Hope. I don't know what these scales are, but over time they formed over my eyes and I couldn't even do the work to pay my tab. Wasted Time tired of me and kicked me out. Unable to see or do anything, I wandered around in Ignorance until Sower of Seed set me on the Path of Life."

That's why he seems so familiar, thought Simple. He had a vague memory of knowing this man in Ignorance. He'd seen him wandering the streets just inside the Boulevard of Broken Dreams.

"I've since learned that when one's sight is not used, it tends to be lost," Hunger said. "The first step of losing my sight was Temporary Satisfaction. That didn't let me see past Ignorance. When that wasn't enough for me anymore, then Lost Hope dimmed my sight till I couldn't even see the next step in front of me.

One day, when I started wondering aloud what existed outside of Ignorance, word got back to Wasted Time and he set his boys Procrastination and Indecisive to beat me over the head and kick me around saying, 'Good Luck getting past the crows.'"

I'm not sure what they were talking about, but Sower of Seed came along to help me, and then later Faith introduced himself to me. All that to say, it appears to me that the King has been providing help all along the way and here you are! Thanks again for being here just in the nick of time."

"I did nothing other than travel the path as it was in front of me," Simple said. "So glad I was able to help. I wonder about the scales over your eyes, though. Hard to believe that the effects of Temporary Satisfaction and Lost Hope would be a permanent loss of vision. I wonder if now that we're in the New Country if there's somehow we could get rid of your scales?"

"When I crossed over from the Old Country to the New Country, the King visited me in a dream. He said we should talk to him just like he's right here with us, that we could ask him anything and that we'd be surprised in how he answers our questions. Why don't we take a second to try it out?" Simple said to Hunger.

"I think that's a great idea. Let's do it," Hunger replied. Hunger and Simple walked over to the right side of the road and sat on a rock under some large branches of one of the trees. Simple looked at Hunger sitting there and he felt compassion for this older man who was unable to see. The more he thought about it, the more miraculous it was that this man had traveled out of Ignorance, past the Stealers of Seed, over Rocky Bottoms and all the way here to this part of the Path of Life in the New Country.

Simple began speaking in his spiritual language, just has he had been doing earlier, but Hunger tilted his ear in Simple's direction with a perplexed look on his face. Feeling a flush of red in his cheeks, Simple thought: *maybe this just isn't quite the right time for that.* So, he sat there for a moment longer in quiet, closed his eyes and then began:

"King of the Old Country and the New. We sit here today to ask for your help. We acknowledge how miraculous it is that both Hunger and I—but especially Hunger—to have been able to get loose from Wasted

Time and to journey down the Path of Life from the Old and into the New. We ask you today if there's any way for the scales over Hunger's eyes to be taken away, so that he can see to continue his journey. If this is something you can do, we ask that you would do it. If there's something we can do, we ask that you would show us what that is."

A dove cooed from somewhere in the tree just above and there was a tangible sense of peace in the air, right there on the side of the road. Now Simple felt peace to pray in his language quietly, so Simple began to meditate softly in his spiritual language to himself. The peace became thick like a cloud of presence surrounding them. Simple wanted to look at Hunger to see what he was doing, but it was evident that this was a special moment and so they sat there, listening, waiting and basking in this presence until a little while later, when it lifted and Simple opened his eyes.

The dove cooed again from closer than the previous time in the branch above them. It was then that a ray of light seemed to awaken a memory in Simple's mind and he had an idea. Was it not just that morning that he had been reading the words of the Book of Life and it had said plainly, "If any two will agree in my name, then I will do what they request?" Getting excited, Simple shared the passage that he had read with Hunger. As he finished, the anticipation was evident in Hunger's face. He wanted to have the scales gone, and so they agreed to try it out together.

"I've never done this before, but it just feels right, so I'm going to put my hands over your eyes and make a bold declaration. Is that all right with you?" Simple asked.

"Absolutely, let's do this." Hunger said.

Simple stood, then helped Hunger to his feet. Putting his hands over the scales covering Hunger's eyes,

Simple declared out loud, "Hunger and I are in agreement, therefore in the name of the King, may the scales be gone and may your eyes be opened to see again, that you might travel the Path of Life with sight!"

To Simple's surprise, he immediately had the sense of warmth under his hands, and so he lifted them from Hunger's face to take a look. There, around the scales he could see a cool, white light like sparks that began to burn around the edges of the scales, as if a spider web was catching fire. That white fire burned slowly, starting at the bottom of both eyes and circled both ways around the eyes all the way to the top of the scales in a circular motion until the sparkling fire reached the top. Then the scales fell and when they hit the ground, they exploded into a puff of ash and dust. A light breeze that had just sprung up carried the particles away. Hunger's bright green eyes could be seen now, and they were lit with such excitement.

"I can see!" Hunger said. "I can see!" He stood up from the rock and began dancing around the dirt path with such joy and excitement that Simple laughed at the hilarity of the older man's antics. After a few minutes of this dancing, Hunger came back excited and desperate to be off once again. "Thank you so much Simple! I've got to get back on the Path of Life and meet this wonderful King for myself! I've heard his fame, I've seen his works, I believe he is true. Now I've got to find him for myself and thank him! Also, I heard that there's a town up ahead and now that I can see I need a Book of Life to read for myself! I'm off and thanks again!" Hunger gave Simple a bear hug, then waving goodbye, turned and ran off down the road with an even greater hunger to meet the King than he'd had before.

Simple stood there at the rock completely in shock and in awe at what had just happened. Once again, the words of the Book of Life had proven powerful to help him in this journey down the Path of Life. Simple resolved right then and there that when possible, he would start each day with two actions. First, he would spend time in the Book of Life, as he was realizing how outward manifestations of hidden truths could happen in his life. After all, it had been proven true that when two agreed in the name of the King, he would do it. Second, he would spend time using his spiritual language, as he was starting to understand how foolish things became wise.

After a few more moments of basking in the wonder of what had happened, Simple stood up and continued on his journey down the Path of Life.

Simple saves Hunger just in the nick of Time

10

GOOD INTENTIONS

Treat others the way you would want to be treated.

Thue to his resolution the day before, Simple got up a little earlier than normal, before there was even light, to spend some time with the King. He spent awhile talking to the King about the previous day, how the experience with Hunger had really stirred his heart for the greater things of the Kingdom. After talking with the King, Simple sat on a rock on the side of the road meditating peacefully as the morning stars disappeared and the blackness of sky turned pink, then blue. Now, with light to see, he took time to read in the Book of Life.

As before, Simple read for awhile until he sensed a clear resonance inside himself like the string of an instrument strumming a beautiful song. This particular passage that resonated with him did so in such a way that it almost jumped off the pages grabbing his attention. He read the passage again and again: *Treat others the way you would want to be treated.*

This is good, Simple thought to himself. *I would think its meaning is clear and that it speaks for itself, but I guess there are many that need to hear and be reminded of this again and again. If I had known of these words, I would have never fallen in with Deceitfulness of Wealth back in the Old Country. Well, let's get back on the Path of Life and see how this plays out today.*

Simple packed away the Book of Life in his leather pouch, slung it over his shoulder and continued his journey on the Path of Life, excited to see what would happen today. The forest opened up with sizable clearings here and there along the path. The shade that the trees had given was now gone. As the sun rose, it became hotter than normal and Simple's clothes grew damp with the exertion of the journey. He began to long for a cool drink of water.

It was just then—when he was day-dreaming about the cool drink of water—that he crested the top of a hill and came upon on a kindly grandfatherly figure standing on the side of the road like he was waiting for someone to join him.

The elderly man looked at Simple, smiled and said, "Hey there, young man! It's always good to see a follower of the King journeying the Path of Life."

"Well, hello" said Simple, wiping his sweaty brow with his arm. "I'm Simple." He extended his hand.

The man took Simple's hand and gave it a good shake as he replied. "My name is Truth and I've been waiting to speak with you. A really excited pilgrim named Hunger ran by here not too long ago and shared with me the story of what happened with you guys recently. Hey, do you mind if we walk and talk together as we journey the Path of Life?" Truth asked with a twinkle in his eye.

"Absolutely!" Simple replied, excited to meet what was clearly another Ambassador of the King. "I'd be delighted to have your company. It's hot today! Hopefully there's a creek somewhere along the way where we can get a drink of cold water."

"It just so happens that the town Good Intentions is just up ahead, and we may be able to get a drink there," Truth replied. "However, I need to warn you that though many of the residents do have good intentions, the town is led by a man named Legalism. Once upon a time, he traveled the Path of Life just like you and crossed over into the New Country many years ago. After starting his pilgrimage by pursuing the King, he stopped journeying on the Path of Life. He has instead set up camp on the side of the road, just up ahead. He's since had a lot of time on his hands, which he's spent devouring the Book of Life. Unfortunately for him, the Book of Life was written for those *traveling* the Path of Life, which allows travelers to be ever growing and increasing in revelation and understanding of the King's words."

"Since Legalism stopped his journey on the Path and is not going anywhere, his understanding of the King's words in the Book of Life has stopped as well. The words of that book that were intended to bring life now bring death as Legalism has turned the statements in the Book into rules and regulations void of the growing life they were intended to be. Over time, many people traveling the Path of Life have stopped their journey as well and have joined him. Their group has grown so much that there's now a whole town called Good Intentions that is ruled by Legalism and governed by his ridiculous laws. They now believe that the rules are the answer to everything. Right and wrong has replaced the King's intent to love and serve others and the townsfolk of Good Intentions believe that they are much better off for it. It's really a shame."

As they walked, Simple listened to Truth's words while looking around. He saw that the grass in the clearings on the side of the path had become very green and beautiful. Simple took this as a good indication, as it likely meant water would be nearby. But then, Simple noticed a wooden sign that read: "Welcome to Good Intentions. Stay off the grass!" Simple could see structures up ahead as well as a large group of people.

"Speaking of Legalism, there he is now," Truth said.

Simple looked up and realized that they had come upon the people he had seen in the distance and it was quite the crowd of people. Their focus seemed to be on what appeared to be a husband, wife and and their young child. The family was clearly worn out and tired, but they were obviously afraid as they stood in front of a large group of people carrying various sizes of bats and staffs. At the head of that group was an ornery looking fellow that Simple intuitively knew to be the man Legalism of whom Truth had been speaking. This man reminded Simple of the really weird guy yelling about the "Path of Lies" he had seen on the Path of Life after receiving Gift Bringer's gift of the spiritual language, the guy who had fallen and been pierced by the cross around his neck.

Like that man, Legalism also wore a cross around his neck. His sharp face spat random saying after saying at the family while interjections of "Yeah!" and "I know that's right!" were tossed in from the crowd behind him. The horde clenched weapons in their cold hands and waved them in agreement with Legalism's tirade.

The woman was stuttering, clearly terrified. "A-all we asked is if you h-had a glass of c-cold water for the little one. We've been on this journey to meet the K-King for a long time and we're hot, tired and thirsty."

"If a man doesn't work, neither should he eat," Legalism spat, looking down on the family.

"Hey now!' Truth interjected. The crowd turned to look at him. "That man has worked harder than you'll ever know," Truth stated as they walked up. "You've no idea what he's been through just to carry his family across the border, much less get this far down the Path of Life."

Legalism turned, looked at Truth, and seeing him, sneered in response. "Look at him, he's filthy. If he was on the King's journey he would know the King's words: 'Cleanliness…is next to Holiness.'"

Rolling his eyes, Truth looked at Simple, then back at Legalism. "The King has never said any such idiotic nonsense. Do you just sit around looking for ways to put stumbling blocks in the path of those on the Path of Life? Those that are traveling on the journey on the Path of Life are pilgrims in process. They might be dirty, tired and broken, but they're on a journey, which is more than I can say for the likes of you. You're not even on the journey anymore! You've simply camped out making life as difficult for travelers as possible and encouraging others to do the same. It would be better if you had a millstone put around your neck and then were dropped off into the Sea of Forgetfulness."

Legalism smiled slyly, looking like he was enjoying the attention. "You just better watch your step! If you slip up, I've got the whole town committee here with bats ready to mete out just punishment. I'll see that you get what you deserve and that you never travel past this way again!"

Not liking what he was hearing, Simple spoke up for the first time. "Excuse me, Mr. Legalism, sir. I don't mean to cause trouble, but what's the big deal with this family asking for water? It was just this morning that I was reading the King's words for myself and I believe he says we should treat others the same as we would like to be treated. If you were traveling on the Path of Life and it was a hot day, wouldn't you like a cup of cold water?"

"Young man," Legalism replied. "I see that you're new around here, but you look like the decent sort, so I'll take the time to explain it to you. We should all live by rules that should govern our society. Without rules, there would be chaos. Therefore, when the law is disobeyed, then there must be punishment."

"So, what law have these people broken?" Simple asked.

"I've already told you! If a man doesn't work, neither should he eat! If these pilgrims were about the King's business, don't you think the King would've seen to their needs? Do you think a King would even want people as dirty as these? I certainly don't think so. If I were a king, I'd only want the best of the best in my kingdom. That's why around here, the grass is green, the houses are well-cared for and everyone, and I mean everyone, has to follow the rules."

"But according to the King, we are to live by love, not by rules," said Truth.

"Whose definition of love, old man? Mine? Yours?"

"The King's definition as He's laid out in the Book of Life. Treating others the way you would want to be treated is right, just as Simple has said."

"Yeah, well, the King's not here and if he were, I'm sure he'd have everyone following the law!"

"Legalism, you really need to let your obsession for rules go," Truth said. "If there's any discipline to be given to pilgrims traveling the Path of Life, then it needs to be done by the King who actually cares for the pilgrims that are traveling. According to the King, we should treat others the way we would want to be treated."

Legalism brimmed with anger, as he wasn't used to having anyone around with the gall to challenge him. His face grew so red that the vein on his temple clearly enlarged with the pulsing of his boiling blood. He was so clearly angry that he didn't pay attention as he stepped back from Truth in absolute disgust. Turning to stride away, Legalism stumbled over a decorative rock placed on the side of the path and pitched headlong off the path into a beautiful flower patch. After lying there for a moment, he lifted his body up up with his arms. He sat upright and found himself face to face with a wooden sign: "Stay off the Grass— Trespassers will be Clubbed Immediately."

In horror, Legalism realized that he had broken the law he had so greatly espoused. A great silence just settled on the whole area. Legalism stood up, stepped back onto the path and looked back to see that there was a large flattened area where the flowers had been crushed. He turned to the villagers and said, "Hey, I can explain what just happened."

All of the townspeople of Good Intentions that had been part of the group threatening the poor family with their bats and clubs looked back and forth at each other, wondering what to do next. Then, in seeming mutual agreement, they took a step forward towards Legalism.

"Wait, it was an accident," Legalism cried. "I didn't mean to break the rules!"

The villagers surrounded Legalism, and then they all pounced as one, clubbing him senseless. When they finished, they stepped back and Legalism was left in a crumpled heap there on the ground.

Truth then spoke up and with a loud voice proclaimed, "The King has declared: 'Whoever gives even one of these little ones a glass of water in the King's name will surely not lose their reward.' Now somebody get this traveling family something to drink!"

The crowd exploded into bustling movement as they ran back and forth, some even colliding into each other as they scrambled to get the family taken care of.

The father of the family lost his fearful and dejected look as he stepped forward to express his sincere gratitude. "Thank you so much for your help, kind sir. As my wife said earlier, we've been on this journey for a long, long time. We've been so tired that we're not even sure if we're headed the right way anymore."

With a short chuckle, Truth said, "Oh you're definitely on the right track. It's through many trials that the pilgrim goes to meet the King, but don't worry. In just a little while, you'll cross over into the Rest of the Kingdom. You just keep reading the Book of Life and you'll have what you need to pay the toll to cross over. You trust me on that."

Just then, a kindly lady with a noble, but humble air brought all of them wooden cups with a large pitcher of cold water. She filled, then re-filled their glasses, which they drank gladly until they had drunk their fill. Once their thirst was satisfied, the poor family was approached by another family with kids, who took them in, proposing that they continue the journey on the Path of Life once they had been fed, cleaned up and rested.

Glad to see the kindness being shared between the people, Truth and Simple turned back to the Path of Life and continued their discourse as they walked. As they headed out, Simple noticed that the "Stay off the Grass" sign had somehow disappeared.

"I've a feeling Good Intentions is going to change now that Legalism is gone," Truth said. "Hopefully, the townsfolk will realize they're on a journey as well and get back into the game. Folks who don't keep going and don't stay in the race get spiritually stale and weak and fall prey to all sorts of worthless ideas kind of like a ship at sea being tossed in a storm with no anchor. They'll find themselves tossed by every wind of doctrine."

"When the King returns, the leaders that ruled like Legalism will be thrown into prison, while those that ruled in truth and love will be promoted."

"Why did the King ever leave in the first place?" Simple wondered.

"The King is looking for willing subjects, not slaves, and it's not till the King is gone for periods of time that what is in the hearts and minds of the people is really known. Those that love and serve others will be promoted within the Kingdom and those that serve themselves will be cast outside the walls to the outer recesses, the place where there's darkness and gnashing of teeth. You see, this is a reverse Kingdom. Those that are greatest here are the servants of all. That's why the Ambassadors of the King are sent back to serve those on the Path of Life, not dominate them and tell them what to do. That's the part that Legalism has wrong. The King intended for rules to be like a school teacher, a guide to the type of things that person does when they serve the King. A school teacher or guide simply directs and shows the way. The rules themselves are not intended to be the authority, used to rule over others and treat them poorly. They are merely to help shepherd them on their journey."

"I was surprised that the judgement was so severe for Legalism. Why did the people respond so dramatically when he tripped and fell into the flowers on the grass?" Simple asked.

"Those who live by the law, will die by the law and frankly, Legalism reaped what he sowed. When you live by the law, judgement gets blown all out of proportion, as though it were the answer to everything. Judgment replaces compassion and the hearts of the people grow hard. That judgement is a reflection of the hardness of the hearts of the people. Where people have hard hearts, Judgment will be unreasonable. Where people love one another, judgment still happens, but it will also be mixed with mercy. It's the spirit of the law that counts, not the letter. Is it good to not walk on the grass to create beauty that others can appreciate? Sure, but not at the expense of hurting the people the King loves.

The Book of Life is only understood rightly in context for those traveling the Path of Life. The town of Good Intentions, while being a beautiful community with wonderful people in it, was simply a misdirected attempt to avoid the Trail of Trials that all must travel to meet the King in person. Legalism took advantage of the fear of the journey on the Path of Life, by creating what appeared on the outside to be a safe and beautiful place to live. I believe that now with Legalism gone, townsfolk will be able to treat others the way they would want to be treated and hopefully there will soon be a harvest of souls traveling the Path of Life!"

Truth paused in the middle of the Path and looked Simple in the face. "Well, Simple, it's been a pleasure to travel with you this day. I bid you speedily on your way." Truth put two fingers to his brow and just like that, he was gone.

Simple turned his head and thoughtfully looked back down the path, where they had passed through Good Intentions. Then, once again he turned and continued his journey on the Path of Life.

**Legalism threatening Pilgrims
with his ridiculous Laws**

11

REST OF THE KINGDOM

*For anyone who enters the King's rest also rests
from their works,...Let us, therefore, make every effort to
enter that rest.*

I t was the morning of a new day, and Simple was
sitting on a large, round boulder in a pleasant rocky
area at one side of the Path of Life. He was
regularly finding these spots to be perfect places to
sit down each day and conduct a little quiet time session.
In these times, Simple practiced the new language that
he had learned from Gift Bringer. Initially, it had felt
awkward and silly, but the gift had significantly grown
on him. While he couldn't explain exactly how it
worked, it was a definitely a sure thing that he had a
greater sense of peace, focus, and energy throughout the
day as a result. Now he understood what Gift Bringer
meant when he had said it was like being plugged into a
source of power, and getting filled up.

Simple had also recently noticed a difference in the
quality of his dreams. He had never really dreamed
much before in the town of Ignorance and when he did,

the dreams had seemed like a jumbled chaos of what could of been the result of too much food and Temporary Satisfaction. But since starting this journey, he'd had several dreams that'd given him very clear directions concerning the Path of Life. The biggest dream so far, of course, was the one where he came to the Border Crossing, but found it was shut down just before he crossed. This insight and understanding regarding his journey had been a great motivator for him to get out and seek this guarded crossing. Simple remembered and processed his thoughts regarding all these events as he meditated in his spiritual language in silence.

After the time of meditation, Simple picked up his leather-strapped pouch and took out the leather-bound Book of Life. The stories contained therein were fascinating and it was still both surprising and amazing how what he read seemed to have application each day. He had read about foolish things shaming the wise on the day he met Giver of Gifts. He had read about how two people agreeing together had tremendous power and then by agreeing with Hunger in a bold declaration, Hunger's blinded eyes had been set free. He had read about how one should treat others the way you want to be treated and then he encountered Legalism and Truth. It seemed that the town of Good Intentions would never be the same and maybe, just maybe the result of people serving each other would result in many new pilgrims on the path of life. This book was powerful in a super, but natural sort of way as it seemed to impart discernment about what the King's intentions for his subjects were.

Today's reading was about rest: *For anyone who enters the King's rest also rests from their works,...Let us, therefore, make every effort to enter that rest.*

It was these words that were about rest that seemed to glow and come alive this day.

To be quite frank I'm not quite sure what that means, but if the past is any indication, I'm sure we'll find out soon. It has been a long journey and some rest would be really nice, Simple thought to himself.

Closing the book, he brushed his hand over the golden tree of life on the front and returned it to the carrying pouch. Standing up, Simple strung the pouch over his shoulder, dusted off his pants and continued his journey on the Path of Life.

In not much time at all, the groups of trees gave way to increasingly rocky terrain. It was just ahead in the distance that Simple saw a beautiful, large lake in which he could just barely see land on the distant skyline. As Simple walked closer, he saw that unless he had wings like the eagle he saw circling the lake, there was no way to travel around the lake due to the sheer cliffs. Following the Path of Life, Simple walked along the rocky shore and came to what appeared to be a large millstone with a gnarled rope still knotted to the end. As he walked past the millstone, the path led right up to a wooden pier that stretched a short ways into the lake. He had not been able to see it as he was walking up, but here at the end of the dock was a small ferry with a stern-looking ferryman whose dark, hooded cloak covered his whole body and shrouded his face in darkness.

Simple walked up to the end of the pier and said to the hooded man, "Excuse me sir, I'm traveling the Path of Life and the path has ended at this lake. Could I get passage across to the rest of the Kingdom?"

The man lifted his cloaked arm towards Simple with his hand upraised and open. "You must pay the toll to cross into the Rest of the Kingdom," he said.

"How much is the toll?" Simple asked. "Well, never mind that. I suppose it doesn't really matter, as I've no money, nothing at all," Simple stated matter of factly.

The Ferryman raised his hooded head at Simple and very sternly said. "No-one in the New Country has nothing. Did you receive the Book of Life when entering the New Country?"

"Well, yes."

"Have you been reading that book?"

"Yes, I have. Every single day."

"Let me see the book."

Simple removed the book from the pouch and handed it to the Ferryman. The Ferryman took the Book of Life, and turning it upside down, began flipping the pages. Out dropped several gold coins! Where had this money come from? How could he have been carrying this incredible treasure that he had never seen before?

"Evidently you have been reading and therefore, you have been provided what is needed to cross over. Have you learned a new language recently?" the Ferryman asked.

"Well, yes I have. Gift Bringer taught me as soon as I crossed over the Border."

"Then check your pockets and you will find you have received even more than this."

With initial reluctance, but then with growing anticipation Simple put his hands into his pockets and fished around in them. He'd thought his pockets were empty, but found that much to his surprise, that—yes, indeed—he did have coins there as well. He took the coins out, showing the Ferryman.

"How much do I need to pay the toll for passage?"

"It will cost all you have to pass into the Rest of the Kingdom."

Simple looked down at the coins that he had just discovered in his pockets, as well as the gold coins on the dock that had fallen from the Book of Life. For just a moment, he considered he could return to Good Intentions or the City of Pleasure, for that matter, and be taken care of for quite a while with what he had here. Perhaps he could purchase the ruby necklace he had seen at the wooden stall during the night at the City of Pleasure—or had that just been part of a dream? He could always continue his Journey on the Path of Life at a later time, couldn't he?

Shaking his head, Simple picked up the coins from the dock and handed over all of his newfound wealth to the Ferryman. He was recognizing a similar thought process that he had when he'd joined up with Deceitfulness of Wealth for a short while. Once past that initial hesitation, Simple was glad to give up the money remembering that there would likely be more deposits coming in the future as he continued his journey. Maybe the deposits only showed up when the time was right and he needed them?

The Ferryman stepped back and waved Simple into the small craft. Simple climbed aboard, careful not to tip the boat as he sat on the seat toward the front. Simple turned, looking back towards the rear of the boat to try to get a better look at the Ferryman, but was unable to see the man's face in the darkness of the hooded cloak. This mysterious man pushed off from the wooden dock with a large wooden pole and began the journey across the quiet, still lake.

"You're not the first pilgrim to come here not knowing the tremendous value of the deposits you had received. These treasures are deposits that have been given to your spirit when reading the words of the Book of Life. Those deposits become reality when by faith you step into a situation where the deposit is needed. You will receive even greater spiritual deposits than these, especially when using the other gifts the King provides as well. You don't always know that these deposits are available or how valuable they are, but at the right time, when you're taking action by faith, you'll be glad that the deposits were made. As revelation becomes reality, they'll help you cross over to the next part of your journey while traveling the Path of Life.

Faith comes by hearing and hearing by the Words of Life. It's one of those mysteries of the Kingdom that happens as you read the words of the King. Although the King isn't physically here at the moment, He's still provided all that we need. You'd be surprised at the number of people who come to the beginning of the Rest of the Kingdom, but have not exercised the spiritual discipline needed to make the deposits into their spirit and are therefore unable to pay the toll to cross. Others have received the deposits for exercising spiritual disciplines, but are unwilling to give them up, thinking the treasure they've received is more important than entering into the Rest of the Kingdom. It's too bad, as this lake must be crossed before one can successfully navigate the Trail of Trials that comes before the final leg of the journey to the Caverns of Zeal.

"Why must one cross the Rest of the Kingdom?," Simple asked. "Isn't there another way around?"

"There is another way around. However, crossing the Rest of the Kingdom turns the Trail of Trials into the Path's of Purpose. If one has not received the rest they receive here in this place, they can get locked away in one of the trials and never move beyond to the Caverns of Zeal."

"I hear what you're saying," Simple said, "but I'm really not getting what you mean. What does that mean, the 'Rest of the Kingdom?'"

"The Rest of the Kingdom is peace, peace like a river in your soul. It's a peace that surpasses all understanding. A peace that's not dependent on the circumstances of life to go your way. When you find this peace, it's like a river of living water that is always available to restore, refresh and wash away the things of

127

this world that try to exhaust us or take us off the journey. When one is able to step into this rest, they discover that the truths found in the Book of Life are treasures worth far more than the cost of time and discipline it took to receive them. Truths that the King wrote in his book, such as 'one handful with peace and tranquility are much better than two handfuls with toil and chasing after the wind.'"

Simple considered the ferryman's words as the boat gently rocked across the quiet waters.

"You mentioned that many people come to the dock, but won't give up what the King has already provided…Why is that?"

"Entering into the Rest of the Kingdom is serious business. To do so one has to give up all that they've obtained. All of the Kingdom belongs to the King; the cattle of a thousand hills are his, the trees and the paths, the rivers and lakes, the Path of Life are all his. Because he is a good King, it's his desire, his delight to give us the Kingdom. That gift, however, is not because we are his vassals and have slaved and worked hard for it— though we are his subjects. He gives it to us, because He's for us and He's excited that we would follow after Him even though we can't see Him. This journey of faith results in tremendous reward, and that reward, if not experienced now on the journey, then will certainly be received at the end.

For some, the idea that our King would make provision for us, is just too hard for them to grasp. They want to earn their passage through the work of their own hands. The King already owns everything, so there's nothing we can give Him that's not already His. To cross over into the Rest of the Kingdom, one has to truly acknowledge that their provision came from the King. Otherwise, they will strive for more and more in a never ending struggle, trying to prove themselves in a way that can never sustain them on the Trail of Trials. Again, there they would remain stuck and their trial will never turn into purpose.

In the end, the greatest lessons are the simplest. Everything belongs to the King. The more time we spend with the King, the more we are able to let go of the work of our own hands and receive that which He has to give, even when it doesn't make sense. In order to accept this, you have to give up all that you've obtained so far. Many are not willing to give up what they've toiled and striven for."

As the boat rocked gently, Simple watched as a majestic white-headed eagle that had been circling above entered into a dive towards the water, glided on the surface at a great speed, then snatched a fish from the lake. A gust of wind blew and the eagle soared up on the wind towards a rocky cliff in the distance, carrying his quarry. The wind blew in gusts again and looking back at the Ferryman, Simple saw the wind blow the man's hood back from his face. To his surprise, Simple realized that it was Faith himself that was guiding the craft across the Rest of the Kingdom!

"Faith!" Simple exclaimed. He jumped up and the skiff rocked so hard it almost tipped over. Simple sat again quickly, not wanting to tip the boat. "It's you!"

Faith now had a sun-bronzed and ruddy face. He was the very picture of health, strength and vibrancy, yet the light wisps of grey in his hair spoke of a passage of time and the gaining of a maturity that transcended Simple's first encounter with him in the town of Ignorance, when he'd been saved from the flock of Stealers of Seed.

Beaming broadly as he dug the wooden pole into the water and guided the craft across the lake, Faith replied with a beaming smile, "Yes, it's me again! I've been checking in on you all along the way. Just thought it was time to show up again to encourage you on your journey.

You're doing great, Simple. You've come a long way from the Tavern of False Fulfillment in the town of Ignorance. I'm here to celebrate your victories and warn you about what's ahead. Congratulations in passing the town of Good Intentions. Many find the comforts of the town hard to resist after the rigors of the journey.

The Old Country and the New Country are really not the point of the journey, as the King's Kingdom is not of this world, but that's why we must stay on the move on this journey, even to the very end. I need to tell you that although you're in the New Country, Wasted Time's not wasted any time trying to devise ways to stop you on your journey. He's got some traps laid out ahead for you, but if you'll stay on the Path of Life, not let yourself get distracted and remember what you've learned, your trials will turn into purpose."

It was just then that they reached the other side of the lake and the skiff slowed as the bottom scraped over the sand and gravel of the shore. They both hopped off and after, splashing through the shallow waters, embraced one another.

"I've missed seeing your face, Faith!" Simple said.

"I've been with you all along the way, even when you don't see me. Just remember to keep reading the Book of Life. As I said before, faith comes by hearing and hearing by the words of Life. Continue to talk to the King like He's there with you and utilize the gifts you've been given. Your invisible spiritual deposits will have outward manifestations at just the right time and you're going to come out just fine."

Faith squeezed Simple on his shoulders, then before Simple knew it, he was gone. Faith's habit of suddenly disappearing wasn't even surprising to Simple anymore. Simple turned and looked out over the beautiful lake he had just crossed. He looked up towards the jagged cliffs and wondered about the eagle's family and if there were little ones now eating the fish that the eagle had snatched from the water.

It was now that Simple remembered the words he had read just that morning, "For anyone who enters the King's rest also rests from their works,... Let us, therefore, make every effort to enter that rest." It was beginning to come together. Faith had communicated that on the journey, sometimes travelers rely on themselves or their own works rather than trust that following the King is sufficient to provide what they need for the journey.

Hopefully, I'll be able to do that when needed up ahead, he thought.

Simple turned back to the land up ahead and walked through the shallow water up the shore. His feet crunched the pebbles into the ground as he stepped up onto dry land and he continued his journey on the Path of Life.

Ferryman at the Rest of the Kingdom

12

TRAIL OF TRIALS

You will not fear the Terror of Night...
It will not come near you.

I t was the dawn of a new day, and the stony surroundings had given way to large trees all around the Path of Life. Grass covered by fallen brown leaves grew right up to the path. Here, on the side of the path, Simple sat cross-legged on a convenient stone, engaged quietly in his spiritual language. He'd learned by now how to get into his rhythm of praying in the spiritual language quietly to himself so that others on the Path of Life who were not familiar with a spiritual language didn't think he was too weird. This time though, while meditating, Simple felt as though the King were right there with him and even opened his eyes once to check. While he did not see the King, there was the sense of being in a thick cloud of

Presence as he moved his head back and forth. Closing his eyes again, Simple returned to meditating for a period of time until the the cloud lifted.

Drawing the Book of Life from the leather pouch, Simple opened and read from that fantastic book, waiting in anticipation for the Words of Life that would come alive for him today.

While he was reading, a passage began to resonate in his spirit as he read and so he went back to re-read it again...*You will not fear the Terror of Night...It will not come near you.*

To date, the closest things that Simple had dealt with that seemed anything like terrifying had all been in the Old Country. Jumping out the window at the Bar of False Fulfillment to get away from Wasted Time, getting past the Stealers of Seed as they attacked, crossing the chasm at Rocky Bottoms, and the dream about the Old Country being destroyed. All of these adventures had been scary, even terrorizing at the time, but nothing he'd faced yet in the New Country had seemed too challenging, beyond facing Legalism, he supposed. Even there in the city of Good Intentions, with all of its rules, Truth had been at his side and had engaged Legalism's follies.

I wonder what could cause terror in the New Country, Simple thought to himself. *When we were crossing the Rest of the Kingdom, Faith had communicated clearly that Wasted Time had laid traps on the path. I can see that I must be careful today.* Simple packed the Book of Life into its leather case, threw it over his shoulder and continued his journey on the Path of Life.

It was a wonderfully cool day with the trees all around providing shade. Simple crossed a rambling creek that provided a cool morning drink as it meandered past to feed into the Rest of the Kingdom. Despite looking for traps, Simple found the day uneventful, except for the coos of a mourning dove above and the whistle of its wings as it flew from tree to tree. It was quite unusual, but this dove had seemed to be with him most of the day. As he walked, Simple began to worry, wondering what Wasted Time had in store for him. The day was nearly past, as evidenced by the shadows' progress from one side of the path to the other, when he finally saw another traveler just ahead. The dove fluttered and cooed from somewhere behind, but Simple picked up his pace, excited to meet this new person also traveling the Path of Life.

"Hello there!" Simple greeted the fellow pilgrim as he walked up behind him. The man turned around and Simple looked into the eyes of an anxious, but familiar looking man with worry crinkles on his forehead and crow's feet around his eyes. Didn't he know this man from somewhere?

The man took a look at Simple's face, then said, "There you are! We've been all up and down this trail looking for you!" Then he called out loudly, "Over here, boys!"

With dread, Simple realized that it was Worries of Life who stood before him. Out of every direction at once swarmed several people and Simple was horrified when he saw who exactly it was heading his way because he was familiar with every single one of them. Wasted Time bounced his way from further up the trail, sweating tremendously with all of the weight he carried. Procrastination and Indecisive came bounding out of the forest from various areas nearby. Even Folly herself showed up cackling with glee and patting her son on the back of his shoulder.

"You finally did something right, Worries of Life," Folly cackled. Each and every member of this family latched   onto   Simple   when   they   drew   near, simultaneously pushing and pulling, tugging him this way and that. The sky darkened even further than it had so far as every crow within a thousand miles seemed to appear at that moment flying in a cloud overhead. The voices of every one of the crows accused and rebuked Simple cawing, "Seed, seed, stop his seed!"

In his loud and boisterous voice, Wasted Time declared, "Well, it's about time we caught up with you, Simple. Did you really think we were going to let you get away that easily? Back at False Fulfillment, I told you that pursuing the King was a waste of time, now we're going to make sure your journey comes to an end."

"That's right!" Folly said. "You should have listened to my son way back in Ignorance and saved us all the trouble of tracking you down. Now you're gonna see what happens when your past catches up to you. You belong to us, and we're not going to let you go."

All at once, every person was again pushing and pulling, cackling and laughing, yelling and threatening as crows were cawing and flying overhead. Overwhelmed by the noise and confusion of it all, Simple found his hope and excitement for the days ahead fleeing. For the first time in the New Country, he despaired. His eyesight dimmed as a mist came over his vision and he sank to the ground as consciousness left.

Awareness returned very slowly with the sensation of bone-chilling cold on Simple's backside and the back of his head. Taking a minute to sense his surroundings, he noticed that the area he was in was silent except for the sound of dripping water that echoed in a way that told him he was in a large, enclosed room. Feeling at least confident that Wasted Time and his family were not in the immediate vicinity, Simple opened his eyes to a murky darkness and began to slowly turn his head. Not seeing any immediate danger in the murkiness, Simple sat up, blinking his eyes, trying to understand where he was. As his eyes adjusted to the gloom, Simple saw that he was in a stone cell and was sitting in the corner of a room next to dirty walls on a floor strewn with bits of filthy straw. As his eyes adjusted more, he saw a rectangle outline and realized it must be a door on the other side of the room. This was about all Simple could see with the help of the moon and starlight that was coming in a barred window up high. He decided he would go try the door to see if it was locked and if it was unlocked, carefully peer out to see what was on the other side. So Simple stood, dusting off the straw from his clothes. Just then, he heard grating sound of metal on concrete and a soft wheezing laughter.

Tilting his head towards the source of the sound, Simple first saw what looked like a dark shadow, then realized the shadow was something alive as it moved and swayed back and forth. On the other side of the room, next to the opposite wall adjacent to the door was a wraithlike apparition. It had disheveled hair, pasty white skin and tattered clothes, and was hunched down in the far side of the room.

Then, the creature spoke in raspy voice: "Hello, Simple, I am the Terror of Night, the enforcer of Wasted Time's schemes. I get called in to deal with particularly troublesome pilgrims like you. I've been assigned to keep you imprisoned here and off the Path of Life. Wasted Time and Folly have adjured me to keep you company till they decide what to do with you. You've come too far down the Path of Life into the New Country to properly be returned to Ignorance, so we'll just keep you here for now, till they decide what to do next. I'm sure whatever it is will be awful."

Terror of Night broke into raucous laughter. "Know this though: the instructions given to me are clear. If you try to leave or break out of your imprisonment, then I'm to tear you apart, limb from limb, and then I'll feast on your body. I am hungry, so please, by all means try to leave! Please!" Terror of Night cackled and screeched with delight. "No? Then, just sit back down. Wasted Time and the whole family will be here at morning's twilight to take care of you properly."

Terrified, Simple sat down, back against the cold, damp wall thinking about his hopeless predicament. Terror of Night was on the opposite side of the room and Simple would have to pass by him just to get to the door. Now that he thought about what Terror of Night said, it was true. He'd come too far down the Path of Life and could never return to Ignorance, and so he despaired. Simple's eyes moistened as he leaned back against the wall.

It was quite a while that he sat there as the light in the cell shifted with the movement of the stars across the heavens. There was no sound other than that of labored breathing and light grates of steel on concrete as Terror of Night occasionally moved.

Time was running out for his journey—of that, he was certain, but he refused to give up and be at the mercy of those from his past. What right did they have over him anyway? Had not the King already paid his tab when Sower of Seed had given the gold royal crown to Wasted Time back at the Tavern of False Fulfillment? Did he owe this family anything other than his disdain for holding him back from the Path of Life, keeping him in Ignorance from all that was out there and interfering with his journey all along the way?

There's got to be a way, Simple thought. *The King has seen me this far, why would he abandon me now?*

And just as he had done every morning, since crossing over to the New Country, Simple closed his eyes and began meditating quietly in the spiritual language he'd learned. Over time, he felt a peace that

that did not reflect his environment, a peace that surpassed his understanding being released like a river in his soul. He also began remembering words that he had read just that morning from the Book of Life: "You will not fear the Terror of Night…It will not come near you."

Wow, the King knew of Terror of Night, had told him about it in advance, but he said it would not come near him. Yet, there was Terror of Night on the other side of the room.

I wonder if the King's words are more true than what I see with my eyes? Simple wondered.

Here he was with the Terror of Night and he was very much afraid of him and didn't want to be any closer for fear of being eaten, but the Book of Life had never turned out to be wrong before. *It said that the Terror of Night would not come near me,* Simple thought again. *But here he was keeping me captive in this cell of despair until Wasted Time and all his family did who knows what in the morning that was fast appearing.*

What if the words were true, though? No matter what I felt, no matter what I saw with my eyes? Haven't I heard that before?…oh yeah, it was the King at the Border Crossing. "The words of this book are true…no matter what you feel, no matter what you see," the King had said. He'd also said,"Fear not, for I am with you wherever you go."

I guess it's time to put the King to the test. Either what the King says is true and everything will work out fine, or this journey on the Path of Life has all been a fantasy and it doesn't matter where I go. Who knows just how bad things will get if the Wasted Time and his family return? Simple thought to himself.

Gaining boldness, Simple stood up. Terror of Night sat up from his haunched position and began pacing back and forth, looking at Simple with a sidelong glance and fury in his eyes. Simple put his back to the wall, on the opposite side of the cell to Terror of the Night and began inching himself around towards the door. Just has he made it halfway down the wall, Terror of Night let out a blood-curdling scream and charged across the room. Simple fell to the ground and crossed his arms over his head to protect himself.

Before reaching Simple, Terror of Night came to a screeching halt. He flailed his hands at Simple, but his fingers stopped about a foot away, just out of reach. Just then, Simple noticed the chain.

He had heard the sound of metal on concrete, but had not put two and two together, that it was related to something that might hold back Terror of Night. Indeed, there was a thick metal chain that was attached by a large link to Terror of Night's neck. That chain stretched across the room and was fixed by a stake embedded in the stone floor in the opposite corner of the room.

The words of the Book of Life were true! There was no need to fear the Terror of Night because he was already bound. He really could not come near him. Well, any nearer than this, anyways.

"You will not come near me!" Simple yelled at Terror of Night. Terror of Night hissed and growled at him, at which, Simple made another surprising observation: Terror of Night had no teeth!

After all the threats and taunts of being eaten, the darkness and gloom of the cell had covered up the fact that Terror of Night did not even have the teeth to do what he had threatened.

With more boldness than he felt, but still with that river of peace flowing in his soul, Simple cautiously continued inching his way past, back to the wall until he was at the other side of the room where he could approach the door. As Simple looked back, Terror of Night growled, then spit towards Simple and stalked back to his corner of the cell, where he dropped onto his haunches with the sound of clattering chains.

Simple turned back to try the door, finding that it was indeed locked. But upon closer observation, he noticed that the key was hanging from a spike in the wall just to the side of the door. Taking the key, he found that it fit perfectly into the rusty lock. As he applied pressure, the noisy and rusty lock first grated, then clicked and sprung open. Looking back one last time at the pile of rags in the corner of the room that was Terror of Night, Simple put two fingers to his brow in farewell and stepped out into the moonlit night. Simple turned and shut the door, leaving that imprisonment behind him. He locked the door shut and took the key with him.

Without a cloud in the sky, there was plenty of light to see by, with the full moon and many stars. Simple took off at a run; away from the single-roomed building that held the cell, wanting to put as much space as he could between him and this cell before the rest of Wasted Time's family showed up.

After some time, he slowed to a stop, not knowing where he was or how to get back to the Path of Life. With a growing sense of desperation, he worried that he'd left the imprisonment with Terror of Night just to wander lost in the woods until Wasted Time's family found him again. Quickly this time though, he called out to the King, remembering how the King adjured him at the Border to talk to him like he was right there with him. And so he did.

"My King, you've been good to me all along the journey to see me this whole way. But right now, I don't know where I am or even which way to go from here. Would you send a sign, anything to show the way back to the Path of Life?"

Then he waited. In the stillness, he looked up and saw a star brighter than the others around twinkle. With uncertainty, he looked at the star wondering, *Is this the way? Is that a sign?*

Speaking to the King again, he called out, "Is that the way I should go?" and in the stillness of the early morning a light breeze rustled the trees. In the same direction of the sparkling star, Simple heard the coos of a mourning dove and the whistling of the bird's wings as it headed in the direction of the star. Simple immediately headed in that direction, winding through trees and following the star when he could see it. When the trees ahead were so thick he couldn't see up, he stopped and listened and heard the sound of the mourning dove and the whistling of its wings and headed on again. As he pushed through a particularly thick area of brush, Simple broke into the open. There before him in plain sight was the Path of Life. Simple began to run, to get as far away from Wasted Time and his family as possible. And so, he continued his journey on the Path of Life.

Imprisoned with Terror of Night

13

CAVERNS OF ZEAL

He who seeks to save his life will lose it,
but whoever loses their life for my sake will gain it.

I t was late the next morning when Simple awoke in a quiet and peaceful, but stony place alongside the Path of Life. His body ached with pains of the desperate flight out of the Trail of Trials. He groaned groggily and rubbed his eyes, feeling his lack of sleep and the pain that came from the attack of Wasted Time's family, the brief imprisonment with Terror of Night, and the race to get as far away from that place as possible. Simple had run through what remained of the night till he'd felt danger was far enough behind him, then had collapsed in exhaustion by the side of the Path of Life, his body taking the sleep it needed.

He yawned, then opened his eyes and blinked through the bleariness to see Faith standing before him, hair white as could be and smile wrinkles of compassion around his eyes.

"Congratulations, Simple," Faith said gently. You've made it past the Trail of Trials," Faith gave Simple a hand to help him up as he struggled to rise from his position on the ground. "You may not understand it now, but your trials have guided you towards your purpose. What your enemies meant for evil, the King will use for good.

Your faith in the King and his Words of Life that are true, no matter what you see or feel, have delivered you from the Terror of Night and of the imprisonment that comes from Wasted Time's family. Wasted Time, Folly, Procrastination, Indecisive and Worries of Life—all familiar to your past—have tried and failed in a last attempt to keep you from the final stage of your journey on the Path of Life."

As they stood there on the side of the path together, Faith continued, "You have reached the beginning of the end of your journey. Some of your greatest trials are behind you, but in a way, your single greatest one is yet to come. I'm here to encourage you that very soon, what was by faith will be by sight and you will meet the King in the Caverns of Zeal." With a twinkle in his eyes and a squeeze on Simple's arm, Faith turned away, paused, then turned back.

"Oh, I almost forgot. The key that you took—the one you used to lock in Terror of Night—give it to me."

Simple fumbled through his pockets and withdrawing his hand, produced the wrought iron key. Simple handed the cold metal object over to Faith.

"I'm going to cast this key into the the Sea of Forgetfulness," Faith said. "That way, what you've locked away, no one else will ever be able to unlock again. Thanks to you, Terror of Night has threatened his last victim on this part of the Path of Life. Wasted Time and all his family will never use that creature to imprison and threaten others again." Faith put two fingers to the brow, turned and just as quickly as he had appeared, he was gone.

Simple sat back down on a nearby rock, feeling pains in the joints of his knees. After resting a while longer and getting a little more comfortable, he entered into his daily habit of speaking in his spiritual language. He needed his spiritual battery to be charged up, as he still felt spent after the long night. Simple felt an immense sense of gratitude for both the King as well as Gift Bringer for the gift of the spiritual language. This was something that neither Wasted Time, Legalism, nor anyone or anything else could ever take from him, no matter what happened. It was his and he entered into it with passion. It took longer than normal today to come to that place of peace that he longed for, that sense of the cloud of the presence of the King being with him, but he did reach it and it was now time to partake of the words of the Book of Life.

Today, it also took a while to reach a place where something stood out to him. But he continued to read and enjoyed the process of reading what at times were now familiar words that he'd read many times on his journey. Amazing how the same words he had read time and time again could come alive on any day at any time as though he were seeing them for the very first time. At times on his journey, a passage would glow at him. Other times, it would resonate like the beautiful strums of a stringed instrument. Even other times, passages from various spots would just fit together in ways he had not expected, like a jig-saw puzzle forming a beautiful picture. Whatever way he received revelation from the Book of Life, it was always like the discovery of precious treasure on a lifelong treasure hunt. Simple still remembered the words the King had said when he'd crossed the border from the Old County into the the New Country: "…you are to look for the precious stones!"

And so, again, this morning was another treasure hunt in the Book of Life. Today, the passage that both glowed and resonated with him said: *He who seeks to save his life will lose it, but whoever loses their life for my sake will gain it.*

It sounds like this is saying one must be willing to face any danger to meet the King and to trust that in the end, the King will ultimately take care of them, Simple thought. *Sounds a lot like the entire journey I've had so far. Since it's being highlighted now, there must be a new and current application that we'll see soon.*

Simple felt a sense of awe and reverence as he abided in the Presence that was around him and chewed on the words he read. When the time was right, he put the book away into the leather pouch, strung the strap over his shoulder and continued on the Path of Life.

It was a beautiful day with a nice breeze whistling through the leaves of the trees. The coos of a dove were heard throughout the day and from time to time, Simple saw the beautiful white dove through the branches. Once, after hearing the rustle of wings, Simple turned his head and saw a dove's nest in the crook of a branch that was just low enough to reach. Simple gently strode over to the tree and peered into the nest. There in the nest was both a small, delicate white egg as well as the shell pieces of a second egg that had already hatched.

Stepping lightly and quietly back to the Path of Life, Simple wondered about the baby bird and where it could have gone. Had the bird grown up and flown away? Had the momma bird taken him to a new place? So precious was the circle of life.

What remained of the morning passed quickly and it was about mid-day when Simple heard the delicate bubbling sound of water over stones. Cresting a hill, Simple saw that there must be a spring somewhere in the path up ahead as the water here was streaming down the

Path of Life and spilled off the path and into the trees all around. There were flowers here in abundance, of all types and varieties. Butterflies fluttered and dragonflies zipped here and there as honey bees moved from flower to flower. The scent of life here was vibrant and full.

As the Path of Life from here on forward was covered with water, Simple wondered how he was to continue. Looking closer, he saw that there were steppingstones to tread on that allowed him to stay on the Path of Life, even though the water was moving towards him. Water only inches deep intermingled between the smooth, round steppingstones and so Simple stepped quickly and lightly, hopping from one stone to the next with a bubbly anticipation growing in his spirit. This was the beginning of the end of the journey; he was sure of it. There were birds in abundance, even deer drinking from the water as squirrels zipped up and down the trees.

As he turned a bend, the Path of Life with flowing water led to the base of a majestic mountain that he'd not been able to see through the trees. It was here that he could see the water was coming from the opening of a cave in the mountain's side. Simple followed the path further. Certainly, this opening marked the entrance to the Caverns of Zeal.

Simple looked to the side in excitement and almost stepped off the steppingstones into the water, startled to see large unmoving figures on both sides of the path. Looking closer, he saw that they were statues of giants with wings, casting their fierce, but solemn gaze from their positions at either side of the path. It was as though the statues somehow had the power to stop any that might tread towards the cave's opening wrongfully. By now, however, Simple knew he belonged to the King, so after a brief pause, he went on cautiously and reverently.

He entered the opening in the side of the mountain and saw that it was indeed a cavern just high enough to walk in. Where the sunlight reached inside the chamber, there were sparkles of precious stones and threads of various gleaming minerals in the walls. As he stepped inside, he noticed that the stepping stones were now gone, and the water covered the entire floor as it bubbled up from the depths of the earth, spilling out and down the path from which he had just come.

As Simple moved forward, the roof sloped down and walls narrowed to a passage heading into the heart of the Earth. Simple entered into the passage and continued on. At first, the waters merely covered his ankles, but as he continued on, the cold water became deeper until it covered his knees. Thankfully, there was still light here that seemed to come from the sparkles of precious stones embedded in the sides of the passage. Eventually, the passage ceiling lowered until Simple found himself on hands and knees crawling deeper and deeper into the heart of the earth.

As he crawled steadily forward, Simple realized that the ground had begun sloping downwards. He could feel the bitter cold on his fingers as he inched forward and the chill sent shivers through his spine. As he progressed, he realized that the water that had first just reached over his ankles and then his knees was now waist high and was piercingly cold. As he continued moving forward on all fours, he suddenly found himself submerged up to his chin. He knew that now was the time of final decision. All he could hear was the sound of running water and its crisp coldness awakened his mind to such clarity that he knew that if he continued forward, everything might end for him. He thought about his journey and his encounters on the Path of Life and for a moment, pondered going back. But what could he possibly go back to? Ignorance was far in his past; Wasted Time and his family were left behind.

Here in this dark place, Simple remembered the words of the book of Life that had stood out to him this morning: *He who seeks to save his life will lose it, but whoever loses their life for my sake will gain it.*

"Yes, I believe," Simple said aloud. "Meeting the King is the greatest treasure and worth everything." Then, Simple took a deep breath and moved forward on his knees. The cold water reached his mouth, then his eyes and finally, covered his head.

As he submerged under the water, he felt as though the weight of the world itself were on his shoulders and he were about to be crushed. Simple began to panic as he realized he could not carry this weight. He saw how small he was compared to everything around him and it dawned on him that if the rock walls around him moved only a few inches, then he would be crushed. He was completely out of control, and panic began to set in with the sense of being buried alive.

Simple began pushing against the sides of the passage and he instantly saw the futility of his own strength trying to move the world around him and that truly all things were held together by the hand of the King. Simple saw that his whole life was like his current struggle to move forward against the flow. He had no power to move the insurmountable things around him. His trying to change the outside world would be like trying to stand up in this tight space and lift a mountain on his back. It was futile.

Simple found himself standing in the clouds looking down on a vast sea of darkness. In the midst of the darkness were lights like fireflies moving and swarming around. Each and every one of these lights had emotions and feelings, pains and hurts, had need of love and thirsted for joy.

Overwhelmed, Simple thought to himself, *Who am I, one insignificant man in the span of time and space? What can I accomplish?*

Even though Simple felt like he was up in the clouds at that moment, he knew he was likely hallucinating due to the cold of the water and lack of air and could soon die. Not able to do anything about the vision in which he was caught up, Simple surrendered himself. As he surrendered, he closed his eyes and found himself hurtling down out of the clouds, propelled by an enormous force.

With the wind screaming in his ears, he fell down and down and down and down. After what seemed to be hours of falling, Simple opened his eyes and found that he was free falling through the blackness of space. All around him in this vast sea of blackness were the multi-colored hues of stars, planets and galaxies. Most intriguing of all was a giant gnarled and twisted tree root that he was falling alongside. The root extended up and down as far as his eyes could see.

This root was as large around as the trunk of a thousand-year old oak tree and had no beginning or end that he could discern. More importantly, it throbbed with life, a tangible, incredible life. Somehow, he knew instantly that this was the Tree of Life, the source of life for all things. Simple intuitively understood that this massive root was the source of all life in the universe and that the life pumping through it was love, pure love.

Simple could see that this love that was without beginning or end was the source of all things, and was what birthed the universe and all it contained. Stars, planets, moons, galaxies, people, plants and animals: they were all made because of love. This love carried in it both an incredible humility and an expectancy of life to be engaged and participated in.

Out of the darkness, a revelation came to Simple: he was forever "falling in love." This concept overwhelmed and excited him; it was indeed worth it all. The few moments on earth, the years, the pains—they were nothing compared to the eternal nature of this life, this love that filled him and washed over him and would forever increase as there was no boundary that could hold it back, no limit to its infiniteness.

More importantly, Simple could do nothing to gain this love, nothing except be out of control and receive it. He drank deeply of love and received it with everything in him. As he did so, he saw how his trials had guided him to this point. Every trial, every temptation he had overcome had been part of a divine pattern that had brought him here to where he was today.

In awe at the simplistic majesty of it all, Simple continued to fall and fall and fall, completely out of control. As he as did so, he received the love, the life that was the source, the beginning and purpose of all things. In the darkness, it seemed as though Simple heard the coo of a dove. He blinked and suddenly found himself hurtling back towards Earth, towards the Caverns of Zeal, then deep into the heart of the mountain.

Ice-cold waters shocked Simple out of his ethereal experience. As he reached out his arms, his numbed fingers found a handhold in the rock in front of him. Grasping onto that spot, he pulled for all he was worth. Like a cork leaving a bottle's mouth, his body popped out from under a dip in the rock. He came up the other side and into an open space where he gasped as fresh, clean air filled his lungs. Treading water, he breathed deeply. As the water poured from his face, he moved a lock of wet hair from his eyes. There, just ahead of him, was a rock that was higher than him, rising up out of the water.

Simple swam across this open place to the rock and was surprised when a hand came down from above and took hold of his hand. With one motion, this strong hand lifted Simple up out of the water until his feet landed on firm ground.

Wiping the water from his eyes, Simple looked up to see who had taken his hand and lifted him up.

It was the King, in all his glory, wearing a jeweled cloak and smiling broadly. The King threw a beautiful white cloak around Simple's shoulders and then He wrapped his arms around Simple. As the King embraced him, Simple felt the warmth and the strength of a father's love. The King whispered into Simple's ears, "Well done, well done!" Releasing Simple from the embrace, the King took Simple by the arms, looked into his eyes and said, "My son, it's so good to finally be with you face to face."

Caverns of Zeal

How Pilgrim's Process Came to Be

The initial motivation in writing this book was to creatively share a very personal story; my journey on the Path of Life. Just like Simple in this book, one of the catalysts in my journey was a real person, my own personal Sower of Seed whose name was Jeff Talbert, my small group leader at the time. Though I was already a Christian, it was through weekly meetings at the coffee shop with Jeff to talk about life, scripture, and to pray that he called me out of the Tavern of False Fulfillment and cast a vision for so much more. The rest of the allegorical journey mentioned in this book was also very real with many practical manifestations.

Fun fact; this book is filled with many actual dreams, pictures, and experiences that I've had through the years. Some of them are as follows…

Chapter 6. - The story of the Simple's dream in the City of Pleasure and journey to find that the Old Country would be destroyed by fire and brimstone, then having the border shut down before passing over was all a vivid dream I had one night. This dream was powerful in my life in challenging me to seek the greater things of the Kingdom, by moving on from the old and into the new.

Chapter 7 - The King's message about searching out precious stones is a spiritual lesson the Holy Spirit taught me about how to receive revelation. Many spend their lives focusing on, pointing out, and storing up worthless stones (other's imperfections, ideologically or otherwise) but we as followers of the King are called to seek out the treasures that are often hidden in the midst of imperfections. It is in storing up these treasures that we find ourselves with the ability to share, encourage and help others with real and practical answers in a crazy world.

Chapter 8 - Simple's steps of faith and feelings of silliness when trying out the gift of praying in the spirit was my experience as well. No bolts of lightning here, but the practice of this discipline has provided some of the greatest personal benefits of my walk with the King

Chapter 12 - Seeing a spirit as having no teeth was an unusually real experience I had early one morning. Understanding fear as toothless does not mean it just goes away, just that its bark is louder than its bite. This knowledge and understanding releases deliverance to move forward in life out of various bondages and into freedom.

Chapter 13 - The picture of Simple falling through space and seeing the gigantic roots to the Tree of Life and experiencing the love of God is a significant dream I experienced one night that released powerful transformations in my life. God's unconditional love can be understood in a very special way when experienced when we're completely out of control and can do nothing to earn it. This type of love is empowering, because believe it or not, it is the root source of Life for the universe. While we were still sinners, Christ died for us. This is the reason that we exist; to receive and experience God's love. In this place of favor that is undeserved, incredible treasures and beauties of the Kingdom are revealed. Over time, I've come to realize that this book is not just my personal story, but is also a prophetic story that I hope is a trumpeting call to all that would hear. In the midst of the shakings of this world, God is calling all of us out of ignorance, out of our places of familiarity, and onto the Path of Life to pursue the King. Some of us may even be unknowingly residing in the city of Good Intentions, using the Bible as a book of rules that are expected to be followed, rather than the Words of Life they are intended to be as we journey in pursuit of greater knowledge and relationship with the King.

Wherever you are on your journey, my hope is that this book encourages you, that your faith grows, and that you would experience the revelation of how the King provides for all of our needs as we engage Him daily on the Path of Life.

About the Author

David A. Harris, Sr. resides in Waco, Texas with his wife, 4 boys, and dog Ellie. In the mid-late 1990's, the Holy Spirit broke into David's life with an explosion of prophetic dreams and experiences. Since that time, it has been David's passion to listen daily to God's heart; partnering with Him in prayer to see Kingdom purposes advanced and following where He leads.

Other Books by this Author

SPIRIT CHRONICLES:
A POWER ENCOUNTER

- A creative, illustrated spiritual equipping book for children that teaches about using their authority in the name of Jesus to overcome attacks of fear.

53314789R00102